DEATH ON THE WAVES

Iain McLaughlin

Erimem: Death on the Waves © Iain McLaughlin
Editor: Julianne Todd
Range Editor: Iain McLaughlin
First published in 2019
Erimem and associated concepts Copyright © 2019 Iain McLaughlin
All rights reserved.
Cover illustration by Grace Prentis
photograph by Dorina Petco
First published in 2019 by Thebes Publishing
follow us online:
www.thebespublishing.com
https://www.facebook.com/ThebesPublishing
https://twitter.com/ThebesNews
ISBN: 978-1-910868-35-5

THEBES PUBLISHING

ERIMEM
DEATH ON THE WAVES

CHAPTER ONE

Warren Anderson was what was known as a gentleman's gentleman. He knew what sort of cheap reaction that title elicited among the lower orders in society and even in the lower ranks below stairs in the Manor, but Warren Anderson had always taken enormous pride in his work. It was his job as a valet to ensure that his employer was impeccably turned out at all times. His tasks also included other personal matters such as preparing pyjamas or turning down beds, and on foreign excursions such as this one could never be too sure of the beds, but it was in preparing his employer – his gentleman – for the day ahead that would decide how well Warren Anderson had done his duty.

The problem was the in this instance his employer was no gentleman, at least not by the traditional understanding of the word.

Lord Carston Etheridge was a scoundrel at best and a beast at worst.

Etheridge had inherited an estate from his father back just at the turn of the century. His father, the previous Lord Etheridge had been a kind, jovial and warm man who had allowed his estates to bumble on as they had for centuries, loved by the tenants who paid him a pittance in rent. He had died of a heart attack, weighed down by debt and worry.

His only son had vowed not to suffer the same fate.

Within a month of his father's death, the new Lord Etheridge had trebled his tenants' tents and turned any who complained out into the street. He had ruthlessly sold any interests unlikely to generate a large income even if they were a vital part of the local community and economy, and he had invested in often morally dubious projects which would generate a quick return. In ten years he had turned the Etheridge fortunes around, but in doing so he had become one of the most hated men in England.

He didn't care.

When the Great War came in 1914, Etheridge was in a prime position to profit from the possibilities afforded by the war. The government needed weapons, munitions and uniforms. It needed equipment. Etheridge invested heavily in those industries, pushing his workers hard and keeping their wages low. For four glorious years, while brave men fought and died on battlefields, Lord Carston Etheridge raked in money, becoming immensely wealthy and powerful in the process. After the war, he sifted the devastation to cherry pick the best opportunities to benefit from the destruction. His interests became global in reach. As the tendrils of his empire grew, he became hated worldwide.

He still didn't care.

In 1920, Etheridge met the beautiful young socialite Celeste Millington. He pursued her relentlessly and when she rebuffed his advances Etheridge turned his financial might against Celeste's father, squeezing the man's businesses until Celeste agreed to marry Etheridge. Six years later, when he had broken his wife's resistance and spirit to the point that she walked into the lake fully clothed, Etheridge bankrupted his father-in-law the day after Celeste's funeral.

In the years since then, Etheridge had continued making enemies. Warren Anderson knew all of that and *he* didn't care. Lord Etheridge was his employer and that was all he cared about. His task was to see to his gentleman's needs and that was all that mattered. He had been with Etheridge for eleven years and in those nine years he had built himself a reputation for always turning out his gentleman quite meticulously. He always ensured that his Lordship's clothes were impeccably neat and clean, that the cut was always at the height of fashion and that his employer was immaculate. He did this despite knowing that Etheridge considered Anderson to be of less worth than a foot-stool or one of the horses he bred at his English estate. For two years, Etheridge hadn't even bothered to learn Anderson's name. Even now he wouldn't know Anderson's first name and he would never care enough to find out. Anderson put up with the insults and the disdain and the contempt because he was a shrewd and wily man. This position would set him up for life, and unlike his own father who had worked every day until he dropped dead at fifty three, Warren Anderson planned to have a comfortable retirement. If that meant enduring Etheridge for a few more years then so be it.

Anderson looked around the bedroom which had been his employer's den for the past month. It was as pristine as it had been on the day they had arrived. His Lordship's bed was turned down and his monogrammed pyjamas rested on his pillow. Anderson would remain on duty to help his employer get ready for bed unless...

The front door closed heavily.

Only those from Upstairs were allowed to use the front door. Below stairs staff had to use the service entrance round the back. The heavy front door closing meant that Lord Etheridge was home. Anderson briskly hurried downstairs to meet his employer. The high pitched feminine giggle suggested that Etheridge had not returned home alone. They had spent the summer on tour around the Mediterranean. More accurately, Lord Etheridge had been on holiday. Anderson had simply gone about his duties in warmer climes.

The young woman, like most of the ladies Lord Etheridge had disgraced on this holiday was the best part of twenty years too young for him. Anderson had no doubts that charm and personality were not his employer's most attractive features. The women he had seduced were drawn to his wallet and title. Hr didn't blame the women at all. He would be a hypocrite if he did. His own interest in working for the peer was also entirely financial. However, *he* didn't face a scandal and a ruined reputation. These women did. Anderson remained quiet, though. They were all adult women and they all – or at least most of them – were willingly sharing Etheridge's bed. Anderson just did his job.

Etheridge caught sight of Anderson coming down the stairs. 'There you are, Anderson.'

'Yes, sir,' Anderson replied stiffly. 'I trust you had an enjoyable evening.'

'I did not,' Etheridge answered sourly. 'You'll never believe who they let into the restaurant at dinner.'

'Sir?'

'Camilla Bradley,' Etheridge snorted. 'Not just her either. She had her entire brood with her.' He humphed angrily. 'It wasn't an accident either, I'm sure of it. You know, I wouldn't be surprised if this wasn't a coincidence at all. I wouldn't put it past that ghastly harridan to have pursued all over Europe just to bend my ear. You know what it was about, of course.'

'Sir?' Anderson replied stoically.

Etheridge hadn't expected a serious reply. Anderson was there so that he could be complained at rather than for conversation. 'She still blames me for her husband doing away with himself. He made a deal.' Etheridge snorted. 'It's not my fault he didn't read the contract. If anyone's to blame it's him not me.'

'Sir,' Anderson nodded. 'Should the lady call tomorrow before we leave, I assume that you will be out.'

'Precisely,' Etheridge agreed. He moved closer and lowered his voice. 'But keep quiet about us leaving on the boat tomorrow, there's a good man. The...' he cast his eyes at the blonde woman who was looking around the house, rapt. 'The young lady doesn't need to know that we're sailing tomorrow. It would only ruin her night.' A wolfish grin spread across Etheridge's face. 'And more importantly, mine.'

'Understood, sir.'

That was clearly enough conversation for Etheridge. 'In fact, you can have the rest of the night off.'

'Thank you, sir,' Anderson said without a hint of sarcasm. It was, after all, gone midnight. 'Most kind.'

Etheridge jerked his head in the direction of the door leading to the staff quarters. 'Well, off you pop. Long day tomorrow.'

'Indeed, sir,' said Anderson with a curt bow. 'Goodnight, sir.'

As he headed for the door to his quarters, Anderson heard Etheridge whisper lewdly to himself. 'And a long night ahead for me.' The voice became louder as he called to the young blonde. 'How about some champers and I'll show you around the old place?'

Etheridge closed the door behind him and headed along the dim corridor towards his room. He had no doubts that the tour would end up in Lord Etheridge's bedroom and that at some time in the morning Anderson himself would be tasked with getting the young lady into a cab to take her home. At least Alexandria was cosmopolitan enough to have cabs. Some of the places they had visited had lacked such amenities and it had fallen on Anderson's shoulders to drive home a young woman who either jabbered that she "wasn't that kind of girl" while trying to draw details on his employer from him, or worse, he would have to see home a tearful girl who realised the mistake she had made. The ones who cried were the worst. All he could do was ignore them as much as possible and interact with them as little as he could. He wondered how this one would deal with the rejection. That was if his Lordship actually let on that he was leaving. It would be like him to not tell the girl at all and simply disappear.

There was nothing Anderson could do about that, but it was another reason for him to hate Etheridge.

The Agamemnon arrived safely in Alexandria. The ship and crew are ready for the embarkation of our passengers for the return voyage to Southampton. It will be a busy journey. First Class is fully booked for the first time in several years. I hope that this is the first signs of an upturn after the crash in Wall Street some years ago. The names of our passengers suggest that we will have a diverse group of guests. That usually leads to a fascinating journey. We are all looking forward to welcoming our passengers aboard tomorrow.

Captain Oscar Hawkins, master of the *Agamemnon*, closed his log and stored the journal on the shelf above his desk. The clock by the books told him that it was almost one in the morning.

Hawkins was tired.

He sighed. That wasn't quite right. He was old and tired.

Oscar Hawkins had been at sea since he was a boy but now,

as he approached the age of sixty, even his love of the sea couldn't disguise that he was getting old. This trip was fine. It was a simple passenger cruise through the Mediterranean and up to England. That would be fine if the weather held, and given that it was the end of summer and the predictions were good, he was probably on reasonably safe waters there. The trouble came in autumn and spring when it was cold and damp. Arthritis had eased its way into his joints. He had been a bit rheumatic-y for years but the last two winters had been painful for him and he had noticed the restrictions in his movements. He had lied his way through two medicals with the company's doctors but had been forced to visit a few other doctors on his travels. The best of those had been a back-alley quack here in Alexandria who had given him a tincture on his last visit which had done wonders. Hawkins hoped he would have time to slip off and find the fellow again before the Agamemnon was due to sail the following afternoon.

There was a knock at his door. Hawkins would have recognised it anywhere. Three quick raps, a beat then another rap. 'Come in, William.'

The door opened and William Carlisle slipped into the compact cabin. He was a tall, handsome young man of around thirty with a muscular physique, short fair hair and blue eyes which usually twinkled with good humour.

'Captain,' Carlisle said with a smile.

Hawkins indicated for the younger man to take the spare seat, an offer Carlisle gratefully accepted. 'Everything in order?' Hawkins asked automatically. He had known Carlisle since he was a boy. The lad's father was an old friend. The apple hadn't fallen far from the tree. William Carlisle was as much of a perfectionist as his father.

'Everything's fine, sir,' Carlisle answered.

Hawkins sighed and relaxed into his chair a little more. 'Then you can call me Oscar, Billy.'

Carlisle winced. 'Even my mother doesn't call me that anymore.'

'Your mother's not your captain,' Hawkins chuckled.

'No,' Carlisle agreed, 'she's a further up the ranks than that. A mother outranks anyone.'

Hawkins laughed out loud. 'I'll give you that.' He sipped at his cocoa. 'So, what do you think your admirable mother will make of young Daisy Brown when you take her home?'

Even in the dim light and despite his tan, Carlisle blanched. 'Sir?'

Hawkins waved the protest away. 'Don't try denying it,' he said affably. 'It written all over both of your faces whenever you're in the same room.' He held up a hand to halt any denial. 'It's against company rules for an officer – and I'd say the First Officer particularly – to consort with a ship's maid, but you're discrete and you make a rather nice couple. Besides, the right wife would be the making of you. And I don't mean a wealthy one.'

'That's good,' Carlisle muttered, 'because Daisy's an orphan without two ha'pennies to rub together.'

'But she's intelligent and a hard worker,' countered Hawkins. 'I've seen her put a couple of chaps in their place.' He nodded again. 'Yes, she's a good choice, William. Well done.'

Carlisle offered a slightly sheepish smile. 'I don't think I had much say in it, Oscar. It was like being caught in a gale and just swept along. One moment we were talking. The next thing I know it's six months later and I'm asking her to marry me.'

'Marriage?' Hawkins pushed his cocoa aside and opened a drawer. He pulled out a bottle of Glenmorangie and two glasses. 'Normally this is medicinal but just this once I'll make an exception.' He poured the whisky into the glasses and pushed one to Carlisle. 'A toast to you both,' he said, raising a glass.

Carlisle raised his glass and brought it against Hawkins' own glass in toast. 'Thank you – from both of us.'

They both took sizeable draughts on their drinks. Carlisle grimaced but relaxed into a smile.

'Neat whisky is an acquired taste,' Hawkins said. 'Your father and I acquire it a long time ago when we were on a cargo run to Aberdeen.'

'I'm still acquiring it,' Carlisle admitted.

Hawkins felt a yawn coming and put a hand over his mouth to stifle it. 'Sorry about that.'

Carlisle seemed to take that as his cue to leave. 'It's late. I'll leave you in peace, sir.'

Hawkins nodded and chose not to argue against the return to formality. 'Goodnight, William.'

'Goodnight, sir.'

The door closed behind Carlisle and Hawkins let the next yawn come. He really was tired. Wearily he began to undress for bed.

First Officer William Carlisle strode along the quiet and narrow corridors in the Agamemnon's crew quarters. As First Officer he had been assigned one of the larger single occupancy cabins. He and the captain were the only members of the crew who didn't have to share cabins with other crewmembers. By good fortune one of the refits the Agamemnon had been through had placed Carlisle's cabin in an out of the way location at the end of a passage past laundry storage rooms and round a corner. Most thought it was a terrible inconvenience. Carlisle loved it. As he pushed the door open he smiled at seeing the small lamp above the bed glowing dully. He closed the door.

'You can come out now.' Carlisle said. 'It's only me.'

The bedclothes were pulled down and a pretty face smiled up at him. Her fashionably short dark hair was tousled by the bed-clothes.

'I thought you'd got lost,' Daisy Brown teased him.

'On a ship this small? Not likely. Besides, I'm an important man. Someone would have helped me.' Carlisle sat on the side of his bunk. 'The captain knows about us, Daisy.'

'How?' Panic appeared in the girl's eyes. 'I can't lose this job, Will. I need it to...'

Carlisle placed a finger to her lips. 'Hush now. It's all right. He doesn't care. Actually, he *does* care. He wished us good luck.'

'He did?' Daisy frowned. 'Are you sure it was the captain?'

'I'm sure,' Carlisle answered. 'We even had a toast on it.' He leaned over and kissed her. 'See?'

Daisy smacked her lips playfully. 'Whisky? The bottle he keeps in his desk?'

Carlisle's head tilted in surprise. 'Is there anything happens on this ship that you don't know about?'

Daisy's nose wrinkled. 'Probably not.'

'Maybe you should be First Officer?'

'The uniform looks better on you.'

Carlisle stood and started unbuttoning his jacket. 'I'm going to be very glad to get rid of it. It feels like I've been wearing it for days.'

'Don't let me stop you,' Daisy said playfully.

Carlisle looked down at the twinkling eyes. 'Are you just going to lie there?'

'No,' Daisy smiled, 'I'm going to lie here and watch.'

'Floozy!'

Daisy stuck her tongue out. 'Aren't you lucky?'

Jack Beehan was not Jack Beehan.

More than thirty years earlier at the turn of the century, Danny Pinner, a Cockney born and bred, had got himself as drunk as could be and had found himself in a fight in a bar on a little island whose name he couldn't even remember. There had been a girl working in the bar. He couldn't remember her name either. A newcomer had put his hand up her skirt and when she had slapped him, the offender had pulled a knife and threatened to cut the girl. Danny Pinner was not chivalrous by nature but the terror in the girl's eyes had touched something in his drunken brain and he threw himself at the girl's attacker. The fight had been vicious as the struggled over the knife. When they had toppled to the ground, Danny had felt and heard the knife slide into the attacker. He had felt it scrape along the side of a rib. That meant it had reached the man's heart. That meant it was fatal.

There was blood everywhere. There was shock on the serving girl's face.

Danny panicked and ran. He had to get off the island quickly. There was a ship leaving the next day and he knew they needed crew. On his previous ship, the sailing of which he had missed because he had been lying drunk in the shade of a tree, Danny had known an Irishman by the name of Jack Beehan. Jack had been roughly the same age as Danny but he had been no sailor. He had regretted signing aboard almost immediately and it had come as no surprise to Danny when Jack had become ill and died

15

less than a year into after signing aboard. Danny had promised to take the letters his dying friend had dictated to Jack back to Ireland to Jack's family. It was a promise he had planned to keep and he had found himself as custodian of Jack's few papers. He used those papers to sign himself aboard the Arrowhead, a cargo ship bound for the Americas, and he adopted Jack's thick Irish accent. Jack had spent hours ridiculing and mimicking Danny's London accent and Danny had done the same with Jack's thick Irish brogue. He was passable enough in his approximation to get himself signed to the ship and when the local authorities came around they were assured that there were no new Londoners or English of any sort aboard. Becoming Jack Beehan had saved Danny's life. It turned out that actually being Jack Beehan was a lot more fun than being Danny Pinner. Women liked his accent. Other Irish sailors treated him like a brother – and those Irish sailors knew how to have a good time. In the United States he could always find an Irish bar full of Irish sailors and homesick girls eager to hear the accent of the old country. Danny never looked back. He embraced being Jack Beehan and loved the life that gave him. Even the accent became natural to him. He didn't even have to think to speak in that accent. The Irish charm he had adopted helped him move onto better ships and into better duties until he wound up on cushy numbers on passenger liners.

The only black cloud was that whether he was Danny Pinner or Jack Beehan he was still fond of a drink. Too fond.

Soon after making port in Alexandria on the *Agamemnon*, Jack Beehan slipped ashore and went in search of a place to drink. It didn't take long to find one, and almost as quickly he found a woman to drink with him. Jack wasn't stupid. He knew the company would last only as long as his money and he also knew that he couldn't afford to get roaring drunk that night. He stayed long enough to get to the point where he felt jolly before announcing to his companion that he had to return to his ship, on which he had by now announced himself the chief steward in the hope the woman would be impressed. She wasn't.

Jack slipped out of the tavern into the warm night. He wasn't sober but he wasn't drunk either. He was in that happy inbetween place where he had control of his faculties but was still quite cheery. He still had plenty of time to sleep it off, too.

Despite still being sharp, Jack didn't hear or see his attacker and wasn't aware that he was in trouble until he felt something slam into him so hard that it lifted Jack off his feet and threw him against a rough wall. He was winded and dazed. He tried to stand but his body was not listening. His attacker was on him again within seconds. He knew that unconsciousness might prove fatal, that he might never wake again, but the pain in his ribs was too awful to bear. It hurt every time he breathed. The darkness was a blessed relief. The last thing that went through Danny Pinner's mind before he gave in to unconsciousness was the image of the real Jack Beehan breathing his last. Then darkness.

Jack Beehan was not Jack Beehan.

Captain Hawkins and First Officer Carlisle were not the last officers to be awake on board the Agamemnon. Ship's doctor Peter Griffiths sat in the office in his little infirmary. In front of him sat a sheet of A4 paper with a neatly typed list of passengers for the coming voyage on it. Griffiths read the list again and reached for the half empty bottle of vodka he had stolen from the supply store. It was over a decade since Griffiths had drunk alcohol. After looking at the list he had every intention of getting blind drunk.

CHAPTER TWO

Despite being named after one of Greek mythology's most powerful men, in daylight the cruise liner *Agamemnon* was rather shabby and disappointing. The ship was more than thirty years old and showing her age. When first launched she had been a gleaming giant of the seas but time had quickly passed her by. White Star's giant ships born out of Belfast's Harland and Wolfe yards less than a decade later had dwarfed ships like the *Agamemnon* and left their accommodation, their upholstery and their fittings looking rather second best, and while these smaller liners still carried the bulk of passengers crossing the Atlantic or travelling anywhere around the world, there was always a sense of disappointment that patrons were not taking passage on board a leviathan like the *Olympic* or the *Normandie*. Despite her modest size and appearance, the *Agamemnon* was a swift ship, and her speed has afforded her a second source of income. Whereas once she had carried passengers in three classes – First, Second and Steerage, the *Agamemnon* had converted the Steerage quarters into storage space for extra cargo. It was a simple truth that goods brought in more money than the poor and was considerably less demanding during a voyage, and so the only accommodation aboard the liner was in carefully segregated First and Second classes.

A crowd milled around bottom of the *Agamemnon*'s boarding ramp at the harbour in Alexandria, Egypt's largest port. Modest as she was, the *Agamemnon* was the largest ship currently in port and that meant that local traders, merchants and thieves would all be on duty. Unfortunately for them, the ship was only in port for a few more hours to take on cargo and board some new passengers.

A party of four had disengaged themselves from the attentions of the throng on the quay. There were three women and one man. He was in his early or mid-thirties. He was an inch or so under six feet tall, his handsome face was of a colour which told of his Egyptian heritage. The woman at his side appeared a few years younger than he. She had the long dark hair and olive complexion of someone with a Greek background. Her name was Helena and the man by her side was Ibrahim Hadmani, her husband of less than a year. If she counted time another way, he would be her husband when they married eighty years in the future in the summer of 2017.

Behind Helena and Ibrahim were two more time travellers, who had slid back through time by more than eight decades to enjoy a voyage aboard the *Agamemnon*. The taller of the two was slim and wore a flash of red in her hair and an anachronistic pair of shades along with a loose cotton dress. Her name was Andrea but everyone knew her as Andy. The smaller woman, also an Egyptian, was at the rear of the group. She wore a light pair of britches and a pale pink blouse. Like Andy she wore shades over her eyes. At that moment her eyes scanned the harbour and then looked off out to sea. Her name was Erimem and like her friends she was a traveller in time. In truth she had travelled through time more than any of her campanions, since that first day she had abandoned her planned destiny of being Pharaoh of all Egypt to live a life more to her own choosing.

'Is it good to be home?' Helena asked Erimem.

The bustle of the harbour was similar to the way Thebes had been on market days. The people still babbled, sun still shone down and the water was still the life that carried trade and people around the land, albeit this was the Mediterranean rather than the Nile, which flowed by her home city, Thebes. Despite the similarities, time had brought differences which were impossible to ignore. She chose not to answer directly. 'I should ask you the same. Alexandria was your home city.'

'More than two thousand years ago,' Helena sighed. 'The sky's the same but every time I come back the city has changed.'

'I understand.' Erimem gave her friend's arm a squeeze.

In truth Erimem probably was the only person in the world who *really could* understand. It was one of the many reasons they had become such close friends. While Erimem had travelled through time to arrive in Twenty First Century London, Helena had lived every day of nearly two and a half millennia, cursed by an immortality her current travels in time had played a role in both foisting on her and freeing her from.

They headed up the long ramp-like walkway on leading up to the ship. Erimem turned and took another look at Alexandria. It was different but it was still Egypt and it stirred something deep in her soul.

Erimem turned away from the harbour as she saw another few figure coming up the ramp behind her, and she followed Andy onto the ship's deck where Ibrahim and Helena were in an agitated discussion with a young man wearing a blue uniform, who looked at her friends with disdain. Erimem took an immediate dislike to this man in blue.

'I'm sure there must be a mistake,' the young man said.

'No,' Helena argued, 'there's no mistake. A suite with two cabins in First Class.'

'Yes, but...' the young officer looked at Ibrahim and Erimem. 'I mean two of you are... well...'

'Is there a problem here, Lieutenant?' a clipped voice asked. The Lieutenant looked to the side. A tall, stylish young man of around thirty with neat fair hair and a winning smile was approaching along the deck.

'No, sir,' the Lieutenant said.

'I beg to differ,' Helena said pointedly. 'This...' she pointed a finger witheringly at the Lieutenant, 'well, *this* seems to have a problem with the skin colour of two of my party.'

'Should I throw him over the side?' Erimem offered. 'With luck there may be crocodiles.'

This new officer smiled wryly before setting an accusing glare upon the Lieutenant. 'You've been warned about this before, Davis. Go and wait in my office.'

'But, sir...'

'Right now,' the officer snapped. 'Move.'

The Lieutenant saluted and scuttled away sullenly.

'I'm sorry about that,' the officer said. 'I'm William Carlisle,

First Officer on the Agamemnon. I'll take over boarding duties for your party.'

'Thank you,' Ibrahim said.

Carlisle nodded. 'My pleasure, sir, and I do apologise for Davis. Some people are...' he faltered. 'Well...'

'I understand,' Ibrahim said. 'I hope we won't have to deal with any more of that.'

'You won't,' Carlisle promised. 'You'll be comfortably aboard when we set sail. I doubt if I can say the same for Davis there.'

'Good,' Helena nodded. 'I'd hate for Erimem to really wind up throwing half your crew overboard.'

Carlisle laughed. 'That won't be necessary.'

'She's not joking,' Andy said sombrely.

The smallest of the group, whose papers identified her as Erimem Smith, shook her head in confirmation. 'I was not joking.'

Carlisle found that he believed her. He nodded at the young steward standing to the side. 'Show this party to their rooms, Williams.'

'Yes, sir.'

Carlisle watched the small group leave, led through the doors into the ship by Williams. They were an odd mixture, he thought. They all seemed intelligent and educated but the mixture of races – especially a mixed marriage – might cause scandal among the ship's First Class passengers. Well, so be it. This was the 1930s and things had to change. He was heading for a mixed marriage of his own... a mixing of classes.

Carlisle turned back to the next passengers. A tall, burly, sandy-haired young man of around thirty, with a heavy limp who walked with the aid of two sticks struggled from the gangway onto the deck. He was perspiring heavily.

'Are you all right, sir?' Carlisle asked.

The sandy-haired man nodded. 'I'm fine, thank you,' he said with an educated but pronounced Scottish accent. Carlisle guessed that the man was from somewhere around Edinburgh. Catching the rail, the young man eased himself aside. 'Please, deal with the people behind me first,' he said. 'I've held them up enough already.'

Behind him was a young woman clearly of Indian heritage though she was wearing western travelling clothes. She had listened to the interchange between the Scots passenger and Carlisle. 'You have not delayed anyone,' she said in a clipped, polite voice which spoke of an education at the knee of an English governess. 'Please do not put yourself to any trouble for me. You should rest your leg.'

Before Carlisle or the sandy haired young man could respond, another Scottish voice boomed. 'Damned decent of you. Just what I'd expect of a good Scot.' A tall, balding man with a neatly trimmed moustache who was a few years either side of fifty but is excellent physical condition, moved past the Indian woman and thrust his paperwork into Carlisle's hand. 'Archibald Mackenzie,' he introduced himself. 'Colonel Archibald Mackenzie.'

The younger Scotsman gave an imperceptible nod and Carlisle quickly ran through the processes of checking Mackenzie's ticket and logging him as having boarded. The Colonel gave a curt nod and followed the young steward Carlisle summoned to take the officer to his quarters.

'Thank you, sir,' Carlisle said to the sandy-haired Scotsman who had stepped aside.

'He seemed keen to be aboard,' the young Scot said. 'Perhaps the heat was a bit much for him. We Scots do struggle when it's above freezing.' He indicated the young Indian woman. 'Please see to this young lady first.'

'No,' the Indian girl countered in a gentle but firm voice. 'Your leg is clearly causing you some considerable trouble. I insist that you go next.'

The Scotsman gratefully handed across his ticket and passport to Carlisle. 'Thank you,' he said to the Indian woman. 'You're very kind.'

Carlisle processed the young man's paperwork. 'Welcome aboard, Mr Dorward,' he said, beckoning another steward. 'See Mr Dorward to his cabin, please, Connor.'

The steward nodded briskly. 'Yes, sir.'

Dorward eased himself over to the side to give Carlisle space to work, but then stopped. 'Could I have a minute, please?' he asked the steward. 'That climb took it out of me, I'm afraid.'

'No worries at all, sir,' Connor answered, removing himself to the side and waiting patiently. Dorward self-consciously settled himself on his sticks and took a couple of deep breaths. He closed his eyes to focus his thoughts. When he opened them he found the young Indian woman was standing by his side.

'Are you all right?' she asked.

Dorward smiled self-consciously. 'I've just overdone things a bit today,' he answered. 'I'll be fine after a bit of rest.'

The young woman returned his smile rather shyly. 'Then you should rest.'

The young First Officer's voice distracted Dorward's gaze from quite the most beautiful brown eyes he had ever seen. 'Connor, would you also show Miss Bakshi to her room. She is in the cabin opposite Mr Dorward.'

'Yes, sir.'

'So, we're neighbours,' Dorward said.

'So it would seem.' She gave that shy smile again. 'I am very pleased to be opposite you rather than your countryman.'

Dorward gave a slight chuckle. 'His country is the army. That's where the loyalty lies for his sort.'

'And where does your loyalty lie?'

The question rather surprised Dorward but he sensed nothing behind it other than curiosity. 'Other than Hibernian Football Club? Recovery,' he answered, 'and hopefully recovering enough to return to duty.'

Miss Bakshi's face fell. 'Oh, you are in the army also?'

'Police,' Dorward answered. 'I'm a detective sergeant. At least I was before I fell off a roof. This holiday has been to recuperate in the heat before a Scottish winter sets in.'

'And has it worked?'

Dorward switched both sticks to one hand and used the free hand to usher Miss Bakshi towards the door by which Connor waited patiently. 'For short distances I can get my on just one stick,' he said. 'When I got here I could barely just stand using both. A month or two and I'll be as good as new.'

'That's good news,' the young woman replied, 'but please use both if you are tired.'

'Thank you.'

Chatting quietly, the pair followed Connor through the door into the ship.

William Carlisle watched them go. He considered himself a good judge of character, and he liked Finlay Dorward and Nadia Bakshi. Unless he was much mistaken – and on a few moments it was hard to be sure – Miss Bakshi and Sergeant Dorward liked each other, too.

A quick but hushed conversation in a heavy guttural language forced Carlisle's attention back to the gangplank, where two women were making their way towards him. One surprised him being younger than he had expected. She would only have been fourteen or fifteen but her voice was deep and she sounded older. The other was perhaps twenty years her senior and Carlisle assumed them to be mother and daughter. They had been speaking Russian so they would be... Carlisle checked the passenger manifest. Yes, he had been right, Countess Olga Bischkova and her daughter, Tatiana. He took the papers which the Countess rather surprisingly proffered herself.

'Thank you, Countess,' Carlisle said with a friendly smile, 'and welcome to the Agamemnon. I hope you will have a pleasant voyage with us.'

The Steward, Williams, had led Erimem and her little party along a few narrow passages and down a flight and rather charmingly faded steps. Their quality was unmistakable, as was the wear and tear that time had wrought on them. Nonetheless, the ship was rather pleasant in its own way.

Williams led them onto B Deck and along to the end of a corridor. There was a door at the end of the corridor, through which was a small hall with two doors leading off of it.

Williams opened one door and held out its key to Ibrahim.

Helena's hand snaked out and took the key from his fingers. 'Thanking you.'

Andy accepted the key to the other door while Williams turned to the door they had come through from the corridor into this little hall. 'This door also locks, so if you want to leave the doors open so you can turn your quarters into one large suite for all of you. He plucked the key from the door and held it out in the general direction of the guests. To his relief one reached out and took it quickly.

'Thank you,' said Erimem slipping it into her pocket.

Williams indicated the open doors. 'Your luggage is inside. I hope you'll be very comfortable with us.'

'I'm sure we will,' Helena answered.

'And thank you,' added Andy.

Williams stood expectantly and there was a slightly uncomfortable moment until Helena elbowed Ibrahim with considerably less subtlety than she had intended. 'Oi.'

Ibrahim winced but understood her meaning. He pulled a pair of British banknotes from his pocket and handed them across to the surprised but delighted Williams. 'Thank you,' said Ibrahim.'

'Thank *you*,' gushed Williams, quickly slipping the notes into his pocket. 'If there's anything you need, just ring the bell and I'll come straight away.'

With that, the steward gave a slight nod and disappeared out into the corridor.

'You tit,' Helena smiled fondly at Ibrahim. 'Have you any idea how much you just tipped him?'

Ibrahim grimaced. 'Not enough?'

'At a guess I'd say it was about six months' salary,' offered Andy. She shrugged. 'At least it should mean we get the A1, top-banana, best service on this tub.'

'I could ask for it back,' Ibrahim suggested.

'Then we'd get the worst service,' Helena countered. 'No, my generous and lovely but financially crap husband, the deed is done.'

'Are you talking differently?' Ibrahim asked. 'You usually use less words to insult me.

Helena pushed him towards the door to their suite. 'Get in there. We should get settled before dinner.' She glanced back at her younger friends. 'See you in a bit.' The door closed behind her.

'Okay,' Andy agreed. She followed Erimem into their suite and closed the door. 'You know, when they say they're going to "settle", they mean...'

'I know exactly what they mean,' Erimem interrupted, 'and it is none of our concern.' She grinned to herself. 'As long as they keep the noise down.'

Andy dropped an arm across her friend's shoulders. 'Let's get unpacked,' she said, 'and then we need to get gussied up for a swanky dinner.'

'Is any of that real English or did you make it all up?'

Andy cackled. 'Wouldn't you like to know?'

The last of *Agamemnon's* passengers boarded the ship at just after three. An hour later the liner eased away from the harbour and began to slip out into the Mediterranean. By seven o'clock, as night began to darken the sky, the ship was moving along at a healthy pace, leaving Egypt's coast behind as a shrinking line on the horizon.

The crew worked diligently, tending to the needs of the passengers. Stewards and maids flitted about quietly and professionally while in the ship's enormous galley chefs prepared food which could have graced the tables of almost the finest restaurant in Paris or London. But only almost. While the *Olympic* could match the finest restaurant, a ship like the *Agamemnon* was a fraction off that standard, though very few aboard would notice the difference.

While their crew worked hard, Captain Hawkins and First Officer Carlisle ran through the itinerary of First Class passengers again, with Carlisle giving the captain his appraisal of the passengers. It was standard practice. It was useful for the captain to know who would be a pleasant passenger and who would be difficult. If nothing else, he would have to invite each of the First Class passengers to dine at his table at least once on the voyage. It would be useful to have some idea of what he should talk about.

With that meeting completed, the officers, like the passengers began preparing themselves for dinner.

The First Class Dining Room on the *Agamemnon* could have passed for a restaurant in any of Europe's capitals. Spacious with a high ceiling and impeccable décor it was the part of the ship that had clung to most of its allure. The table-cloths gleamed a brilliant white, the cutlery shone under the chandeliers' warm light and the furniture offered a sense of glamour from before the Great War had changed the world.

The diners were as immaculately turned out as the Dining Room itself. The gentlemen all wore black tie or dress uniform and the ladies wore an assortment of dresses reflecting the height of 1934 fashion.

The great art deco clock on the wall had not yet clicked around to half past seven. There were still a few minutes to go which meant that several of the tables were as yet unoccupied. It was always fashionable to be late and make a grand entrance, especially on the first night of a voyage.

Stewards flanking the wide double doored entrance to the Dining Room gave a formal but friendly greeting as a party of four entered. While Ibrahim looked dapper in a tuxedo, the three women of the group wore dresses copied directly from the fashion houses of Paris in 1934. Helena shimmered in teal, Andy's dress had silver flecks through black giving the twinkling effect of stars in a clear sky and Erimem was dressed in midnight blue which also shimmered as golden strands caught the light.

'Well, everybody's looking at us,' Ibrahim said quietly.

'Of course they are, dear,' Helena answered happily. 'We're gorgeous. Well,' she corrected, '*we* are. You're simply presentable.'

Ibrahim laughed. 'Why did I marry such a mean-spirited woman?'

'Because we told you to?' suggested Erimem.

One of the Dining Room stewards approached and gave a curt bow, ending the conversation. 'The Hadmani party?' he asked. When Helena confirmed the fact the steward ushered them forward. 'Let me show you to your table for tonight.'

There were seven tables of varying size in the Dining Room. An older man in a captain's uniform sat at the most prominent table. Three of the eight seats at the Captain's Table were still empty.

There was another table for eight, four set for six and a smaller which had placings for just four.

The steward led Erimem and her party to the second table for eight. The First Officer who had taken over their boarding duties was already seated at the table talking with a very attractive young Indian woman. Her dress was a charming mixture of high fashion from Europe and traditional cuts. Also at the table but not entering into the conversation was a little bull of a man with closely cropped hair and an extraordinarily thick and well-tended moustache.

'German,' Andy said under her breath. 'Anybody want to take a bet?'

'Of course he's German,' Helena answered quietly. 'He's copying President von Bismark's 'tache.'

'It's a rasper,' Ibrahim nodded appreciatively. 'I could never grow one like that.'

'Not if you ever want to kiss me again,' Helena agreed. 'That would tickle.'

First Officer Carlisle stood to greet the small group. 'Good evening,' he said warmly. 'I'm afraid you'll have to put up with me at dinner tonight.'

As the only man in the party, Ibrahim was expected by custom to answer first. He restricted himself to a cheerful 'I'm sure we'll survive.'

Helena picked up the conversation. 'How nice to see you again, and thank you for your actions earlier.'

'I apologise for our former crewman,' Carlisle said. He indicated the seats, clearly eager to move the conversation on. 'Our stewards have alternated men and women around the table. I trust that's agreeable to everyone?'

'Absolutely,' Andy answered.

'Capital,' beamed Carlisle. He guided his guests to their sets and gallantly slid the chairs in for the ladies, unaware that his actions were the cause of the smiles and hidden smirks on the faces of the party of four.

'We seem to be a man short,' Helena said, indicating the empty chair between herself and the attractive young Indian woman.'

'We are indeed,' Carlisle agreed. 'I was saving the introductions until the gentleman arrived but here he is now.'

A young man walking with the aid of a single stick made his

way slowly towards them accompanied by a steward.

'Mr Dorward,' the Indian girl said with a slight smile.

Carlisle nodded. 'Indeed, Miss Bakshi. I saw you and Mr Dorward conversing earlier and thought it might be agreeable for you both to know someone at your table tonight.'

'Thank you,' said Nadia Bakshi. 'That was very kind of you.'

The young man dropped into his chair with some relief. He was red in the face and out of breath.

'Welcome,' said Carlisle, avoiding the man discomfort. 'Now that we're all here, perhaps I should introduce everyone.'

Erimem had been quietly scanning the room, taking in the room and the people. Carlisle's suggestion snapped her back to the moment at hand. 'Please do,' she said. 'It is much easier to hold a conversation when we know who we are talking with.'

Andy and the rest of Erimem's friends would have recognised that as her being in politician mode, making small talk while wearing a smile that didn't quite reach her eyes.

Any hesitancy on Erimem's part was either lost on Carlisle or he ignored it. 'As you know – at least I hope you know – I am First Officer, Lieutenant William Carlisle. To my right, Miss Erimem Smith of London, then Ibrahim Hadmani.'

'Also of London,' Ibrahim interjected. 'Believe it or not I miss the rain when I'm away too long.'

There was nothing more resolutely British than a comment about the weather to bring a sense of ease to the introductions. Carlisle continued, 'Then his wife, Mrs Helena Hadmani.'

'*Doctor* Helena Hadmani,' Helena corrected in a gentle but firm tone. 'I worked long enough for the qualification so I'm not giving up the title.'

That drew laughs from around the table except from the man with the thick moustache who snorted, clear in his disapproval. Manners demanded that he was ignored and he duly was.

Carlisle continued the introductions. 'Mr Finlay Dorward of Edinburgh.

'Amazing city,' Andy said appreciatively. 'One of my favourite places to get...' she stopped at the sight of Helena's rising eyebrows. '...an education,' she finished slightly lamely. 'Wonderful place for an education.'

'I have to agree with that,' Dorward said, 'though most of my

time with students was spent arresting them for various hi-jinks.'
He nodded at his leg. 'Before the accident.'

'A policeman?' Ibrahim asked.

Andy laughed. 'We'd better be on our best behaviour.'

Carlisle continued, pleased with the way the table was
already showing signs of relaxing. 'Then it's Miss Bakshi...'

'Nadia,' the Indian lady interrupted gently, 'and at the
moment even I am not sure where I should call home.' She
seemed untroubled by the admission.

'Then you are a citizen of the world,' Helena said jovially,
'welcome and at home everywhere.'

'Shouldn't everyone be welcome and at home everywhere?'
asked Nadia.

'A good point eloquently made,' Helena agreed. 'I think
you're going to be a most enjoyable dinner companion.'

'You're never that nice to us,' Andy said, pretending to sulk.

'That's because she has heard our jokes already,' Erimem
interjected.

Andy shrugged. 'Fair enough.'

'Beside Miss Nadia,' continued Carlisle is our second medic
at the table, Doctor Hans Klimt.'

'My doctorate is in philosophy,' snapped Klimt angrily. 'I
am not a medical doctor.' He spat the final words out as if they
were a curse.

The table immediately fell into an uneasy silence, the
bonhomie killed.

Carlisle recovered swiftly and moved to cover the
embarrassment spreading around the table. 'I'm terribly sorry,
Doctor Klimt,' he said. 'That was an unforgivable error on my
part. I trust you will accept my apology.'

Dr Klimt looked very much like he wanted to refuse the
apology but etiquette demanded that he accept and so he nodded
gruffly. 'Of course,' he said brusquely. 'Of course.'

'Thank you,' said Carlisle with a charm that was a bit too
forced.

Andy took pity on the First Officer and threw him a rescue
line. 'Don't forget me,' she said, smiling. 'Everyone else is far
more interesting than I am but I am at the very least here.'

'And unforgettable,' Erimem added with pantomime

sincerity.

Andy returned the banter. 'Aw, bless. You're a star.'

Erimem wrinkled her nose and smiled. 'I know,' she answered.

'Sergeant Dorward,' Helena said, turning to the young Scot next to her, 'would you mind if I exercised my curiosity about the injury to your leg? You said it was an accident.'

A wry smile crept across the policeman's face. 'Well, I didn't fall off the roof deliberately,' he chuckled. His face scrunched up ruefully. 'Chasing a villain across a garage roof in Edinburgh wouldn't be an easy thing at the best of times. When rain has fallen on frost in the middle of a winter night... well, that's not the best of times.' A smile was forced onto his face. 'But I'm on the mend and I'm in good company so this is the best of times.'

'You arrived with only one stick,' said Nadia. 'Surely that is a sign you are recovering.'

'Or stupid,' Dorward offered. 'I felt adventurous,' he admitted.

Helena switched to doctor mode. 'Most doctors will tell you to use two until you don't need to, but I generally find that if you can manage with just one, you should use one until you really need both. You're walking so your bones have recovered. I imagine that it's muscle and soft tissue that need to recuperate now. The single stick will help you push the muscles to regain strength.'

'I'll take your advice, Doctor Hadmani,' Dorward nodded. 'How much do I owe you for the consultation?'

Helena laughed. 'It's Helena, and the advice was on the house.'

'Got to love the NHS,' Ibrahim added.

Helena patted Ibrahim's hand. 'There's isn't an NHS yet, dear. It's still just an idea of Nye Bevan's,' she added to the rest of the table. 'I think it could be a winner.'

'Gets my vote,' Andy chimed in.

That brought another snort from Klimt, who unsuccessfully tried to disguise it as a cough.

'Something caught in your throat there?' Helena asked genially.

'No,' Klimt asserted. 'I am fine.'

31

'I think we have a goddess among us.' Andy's eye had been drawn to the door where a tall young woman had just arrived. She was tall and slim with fine features. Her hair and dress reeked of money. The jewellery said it was old money. Beside her was another young woman of around twenty five whose clothing was stylish enough but couldn't compete with her dazzling companion. Andy glanced at Erimem apologetically. 'Sorry, *another* goddess.'

The two women were being escorted towards the Captain's Table. 'Who is she?' Erimem asked.

Carlisle quickly provided the answer. 'Miss Penelope Banks. I believe she is something of a fixture in the society pages of the London press. I'm surprised you haven't heard of her, what with you being in London.'

'We're not great followers of the social scene,' Helena explained with a smile. 'We don't pay much attention to who is famous in the papers.'

'I do not understand the obsession with fame,' Erimem said with a frown. 'I understand that people who show great skill in their professions should be recognised. Doctors, artists...'

'Soldiers?' suggested Andy with a wink.

Erimem smiled warmly, accepting the compliment. 'Yes, great soldiers are worthy of praise and glory. They earn it. In newspapers I see people who do little of worth but who are lauded for it – or even more confusing, who are famous only for being famous.'

'The word "legend" has changed,' Helena mused. 'Once it was Julius Caesar or Robert the Bruce. Now it's anyone who manages three weeks in the Big Brother house.' She looked up self-consciously at the rest of the table. 'Please forgive us. We're being unforgivably rude by making references you won't know.'

'Helena is right,' Erimem agreed. 'I also apologise.'

'Think nothing of it,' Carlisle said easily.

For the first time Klimt was actually interested in his companions and their conversation. 'You raise an interesting point,' he said. 'Fame is a fascinating psychological drug. For some it is an escape from poverty. That is a physical matter and worthy of study in its own right, but for others a dream of being famous is a search for acceptance and love they do not find elsewhere, a way to fill their yearning for a sense of worth in themselves, a need to feel important. It is a fascinating subject.'

'Isn't everyone important?' Nadia Bakshi asked.

Klimt snorted and ignored the question as if it was too stupid to deserve a response. 'One day I shall make a study of this.'

Dorward took offence at the blatant snub to Nadia. 'The lady asked a question,' he said.

Nadia interjected quickly. 'Please, let it go. It was not a question requiring an answer.'

A reluctant nod came from Dorward, allowing Nadia to push the conversation back to calmer waters. 'Why is the lady so famous?' she asked.

'Family,' answered Carlisle. 'She is possibly the richest single woman in England. Her father was one of the most prominent industrialists in the Empire before the fates turned against him and when he passed what was left of his fortune fell to her.'

Erimem nodded, carefully appraising the woman. 'Does she now run his businesses?'

It was Dorward who answered. 'No, she spends his money, and gets in the papers for that, and for whatever rich twit whose proposal she has turned down this time.'

Nadia Bakshi's head tilted curiously. 'You seem to know the lady quite well.'

Dorward tapped his stick. 'I was laid up for seven months and only had the newspapers to keep me entertained. I know far too much about things in which I have less than no interest.'

'I'm not surprised she's not interested in the proposals,' Andy said quietly.

Nadia nodded. 'There are men who will only see her money. She is right to be wary.'

Erimem's eyebrow rose. 'You sound as if you speak from experience.'

'All life is experience, is it not?' Nadia replied.

Erimem was unconcerned by the evasion. 'That was a politician's answer,' she smiled.

'Erimem is very good at those herself,' Andy chimed. 'I'd pay good money to see her as Prime Minister.'

'A woman Prime Minister?' Carlisle guffawed. 'I don't think

that's very likely.'

Four pairs of eyes bored into Carlisle, who realised very quickly that he had mis-spoken.

It was Helena who asked the question. 'And why, pray tell, is that, Mr Carlisle?'

'Well...' Carlisle flustered under the intense scrutiny.

'Yes?' Erimem added.

Andy shook her head, refusing the First Officer's silent plea for help. 'You're on your own, shipmate.'

'Well,' Carlisle blustered, 'there are very few women in Parliament.'

'Elect more,' Erimem said quickly.

'But they have duties in the home,' Carlisle protested.

'We're very good at multi-tasking,' Andy replied.

'And,' Helena added, 'there's always the wild and crazy thought that men could do their bit about the home. Cooking and cleaning...'

'And raising children,' Andy added. 'Don't forget the ankle-biters.'

'But men have work to do,' Carlisle said.

'So do women,' Erimem said mildly. 'Helena is a doctor. Andy and I both work at the university.'

Nadia Bakshi enjoyed a laugh. 'Mr Carlisle, I believe you are losing this argument.'

'Well,' Carlisle conceded, 'times do change, I suppose.'

Helena nodded. 'Indeed they do.'

'Indeed they do not!' Klimt exploded angrily. 'Men are stronger, more intelligent and naturally dominant.'

Andy sat up straight, the hairs on her neck bristling. 'Are they indeed?'

'Yes!' Klimt snapped. 'Natural superiority among genders is as clear as it is among races. There must be a natural order.'

'Or how can you have a master race?' Helena asked coldly. 'There has to be someone to subjugate so you can feel superior.'

The German's eyes narrowed and he glared viciously at Helena. 'The English understand subjugation better than most.'

'First thing,' Helena said, 'is that I'm not English.'

'And secondly,' Andy interjected, 'while I am British I'm aware that our history has moments of shame as well as those of triumph, particularly when it comes to the Empire.'

'So you are ashamed of your own country?' Klimt said sharply.

Andy nodded. 'By its politicians and the idiots who listen to them... pretty regularly at the moment.'

'But I'd imagine you would understand that,' Helena said carefully picking her words, 'given the nature of politics in Germany at the moment.'

The atmosphere around the table had become noticeably cold. Carlisle tried to put the conversation back on track. 'My mother always told me not to discuss religion and politics at the table. Perhaps, Mr Dorward, you could tell us where you have visited on your recuperation?'

'Not yet,' Klimt said sharply. 'I was asked a question and manners demand that I answer.' He stared at Helena with cold eyes. 'No, *Doctor Hadmani*, I am not ashamed of my country or of its Chancellor. I am ashamed of the cowards who allowed us to be reduced to the shadow of the nation we were. I trust that Chancellor Hitler will make Germany the great and powerful country it once was. The country it should be. A country to be respected.'

'Or feared,' Helena countered.

'Fear and respect often go together.'

'Or are confused for each other,' Helena countered. 'Usually by people undeserving of either.'

Are you suggesting the Chancellor is undeserving of respect of either?'

'Oh, he should be feared,' Helena said coldly. 'His kind are always to be feared.'

Klimt's self-control was wavering. '*His kind?*'

'Lunatics,' Helena answered. 'Only lunatics would burn books or declare a religion to be a danger or make eugenic sterilisation national policy.' She paused very deliberately. 'Lunatics.'

Klimt's hand tightened around the handle of a knife until the knuckles turned white. 'You talk a great deal on things about which you know nothing.' He fairly spat the last word.

Helena's gaze didn't waver. 'Don't I just?'

Klimt fought back. 'Perhaps your lack of manners are to be

expected.'

'Steady on now,' protested Carlisle, but Erimem caught his arm.

'Do not interfere,' she said. 'Helena can handle her own battles.'

Helena peered across the table at Klimt. 'Why is it to be expected?' she asked. 'Because I am a mere woman and therefore know nothing or because I married a man of colour?' Klimt's chin lifted defiantly. 'That's it, isn't it?'

'You are a loud, rude, ignorant woman,' Klimt enunciated carefully.

'It's all right.' Helena held up a hand to stop anyone reacting. 'I wear an insult from a Nazi as a badge of honour.'

Klimt glared angrily across the table.

'Let go of the knife,' Erimem said quietly. 'I will not tell you twice.'

The threat sat over the table for a long moment before Klimt released the knife and pushed back his chair. 'Mr Carlisle, my appetite has deserted me.'

The German turned and strode from the Dining Room. Helena watched him leave before she relaxed and reached for a glass. 'It's times like this I wish I smoked,' she breathed.

Erimem leaned forward, her face alive with curiosity. 'Now will you tell us what that was about?'

Carlisle adopted a far more formal tone. 'I think I should ask for an explanation as well,' he said. 'That was...'

'Utterly deliberate,' said Dorward, who had watched the exchange quietly. 'You wanted to push him to show his colours.' He gave a wry smile. 'Although I think colours may be the wrong word to use.'

'Or all too accurate,' Helena smiled. She glanced towards Carlisle and explained. 'Doctor... Professor... Whatever Klimt was offended by being at a table with people of colour. In particular with a mixed marriage couple.'

Carlisle shifted uneasily in his chair. 'I'm sure that wasn't the case...'

Dorward interrupted gently but firmly. 'And I'm sure it was.' He gave Helena a brief nod of agreement. 'I saw the same looks he gave people. He tried to hide them but I saw them.'

Carlisle shook his head blankly. 'I didn't see anything.'

The First Officer's protest fell on deaf ears.

Erimem said firmly 'If Helena tells me she saw this in him then that is enough for me.'

'And me,' agreed Andy. 'Besides, I did notice Sergeant Dorward giving Herr Looney-Tunes the evil eye.'

'Spotting people who might turn out to be villains is part of my job,' Dorward said, 'and there was something not right about him from the moment I sat down.' He gave Miss Bakshi an apologetic smile. 'I'm afraid Doctor Hadmani... Helena,' he corrected himself, 'I'm afraid Helena is correct. He doesn't like anyone who isn't white.'

Nadia Bakshi looked upset and then steeled herself. 'Then it is for the best that he is gone or I might have lost my appetite instead, and I am quite ravenous.'

Carlisle took that as a sign to move the conversation on. 'Then I shall make sure he is not seated with you or anyone else who might...'

'Offend him?' offered Andy sarcastically. 'Should we really be worried about offending a bigot?'

'Anyone else who might be troubled by his views,' Carlisle finished. Nobody believed that had been what he had intended to say. 'Some people do have these views,' he went on. 'There's nothing we can do about them.'

'Well, that's bollocks,' Andy stated.

'Andy...' Helena said in warning, but Erimem interrupted.

'Such opinions must be confronted head on. I know you believe the same, Helena.'

'I do,' Helena agreed, 'but I also think I have spoiled everyone's dinner quite enough and we should allow Mister Carlisle to go back to telling us who everyone is.'

Erimem agreed but with a look that said she would return to the matter later and in private.

Carlisle breathed a sigh of relief. The voyage had started badly but it did seem to be returning to calmer waters.

Nadia Bakshi opened the door for Carlisle. 'May I ask, who is that attractive woman? The one with a younger girl and some splendid jewels.'

Carlisle smiled broadly. 'That is Countess Olga Bischkova

and her daughter Tatiana.'

'A countess, eh?' Andy seemed impressed. 'Tell us more.'

CHAPTER THREE

After what had been the shakiest of starts, dinner aboard the *Agamemnon* proved to be a rather splendid affair. With Professor Klimt no longer there to ruin the mood, everyone relaxed, talked and laughed a good deal. The food was exceptional, the wine first rate and the company even better.

It transpired the First Officer William Carlisle was something of a gossip and was happy to explain who everyone aboard was. No-one had any doubts that the next night his guests at table would be informed that he had detected a definite spark between Miss Bakshi and Sergeant Dorward.

He was an entertaining narrator, delivering his descriptions with gusto.

'Countess Bischkova is actual Russian royalty,' he said. 'She was a distant cousin of the Tsar. You know that he and his family were all killed in the Revolution.'

'That's what the history books say,' Andy agreed.

'Mindless slaughter,' Erimem said angrily.

Nadia agreed. 'It was a vile thing that happened.'

The young Indian woman had no way to know that the party with whom she was enjoying a convivial dinner had actually been in Russia at the time of the Tsar's execution and had helped one of the Tsar's daughters to escape to a new life in the United States, albeit without any memories of her previous life as a member of a royal house.

Carlisle cheerfully continued his tale, 'Apparently the Countess was holidaying on a yacht when the Revolution came. She was in her late teens but instructed her crew to perform a couple of daring rescues to get a few her family out of the country and onto her boat. Just the ones closest to the coast, you understand, but it was quite the feat of derring-do. They had quite a bit of trouble finding a place that would take them in. The Russkies wanted them back to stand trial for something or other. They wound up in Singapore, or was it Shanghai, and had a rather tough time of it for a while. It was more difficult for her because she'd just married and her husband was killed back in Russia. They had to sell the yacht and their possessions to make ends meet, but it seems to have turned out rather well in the end. Her daughter, Tatiana, is the young girl with her.'

'She looks like her mother,' Andy commented.

'She looks *after* her mother,' Erimem added. 'There is a very deep and strong emotional bond between them.'

'I see it,' Helena agreed.

'Tell me about my loudmouthed countryman,' Dorward suggested. 'He's boring the very devil out of that poor woman he's sitting with.'

At a table nearby, the burly Scot who had earlier pushed past Nadia and Dorward was now seated at a table next to a rather mousey looking woman, who could have been rather beautiful if she hadn't chosen to make her clothes, hair and make-up the drabbest they could possibly be.

'Colonel Archibald Mackenzie,' Carlisle supplied easily. 'Apparently he has been out in Egypt with the army since the end of the Great War. He hasn't been back to England...'

'Britain,' Dorward corrected automatically.

Carlisle accepted the amendment without complaint. 'He hasn't been back to Britain since he left in 1916.'

'Why is he returning now?' asked Erimem. 'Retirement?'

'I have no idea,' Carlisle admitted. 'I asked him when I met him ciming in to the Dining Salon. He told me to mind my own business.' He coughed discreetly. 'With a few colourful adjectives in there as well.'

'The cad,' Helena joked, sipping at a rather splendid 1904 vintage.

'It could be something military and hush-hush, of course,' Carlisle wondered aloud.

'Then why would he wear a uniform?' Sergeant Dorward and

Erimem asked almost in unison.

Andy put her glass down. 'That was freaky. Don't ever do that again. I'm not drunk enough for that to be incredibly funny yet.'

'He also seemed offended that he was not at the Captain's table,' Nadia added lightly. 'He was rather unpleasant to you, Mr Carlisle.'

Carlisle spread his hands wide to show he wasn't offended. 'Water off a duck's back,' he said. 'It was nothing.'

'Who is the woman he is boring to death?' Erimem asked. 'She looks as if she would happily throw herself into the sea.'

'That's Mrs Rollins,' said Carlisle. 'She was widowed about six months ago and is travelling to get over her bereavement.'

'Poor woman,' Andy muttered. 'As if she hasn't suffered enough already. She'll be looking forward to meeting up with her hubby again if Colonel Boredom carries on like that.'

Erimem's eyebrow lifted. 'Are you sure you're not drunk?'

'Bad taste?' Andy asked.

Erimem nodded. 'A little.'

Andy sniffed. 'Then I'm not drunk. If I was blotto I wouldn't accept the idea that I had done or said anything tasteless.'

'That's true,' Ibrahim agreed.

'Hey,' Andy protested. 'You're the nice one. You're supposed to stick up for me.'

'Three words against which you have no defence,' Helena said. She counted from three to one and then Ibrahim and Erimem joined her in a chorus of 'Vuskin's genuine Copacabana.'

Andy winced. 'Okay. You win. I did go the full Manilow, didn't I?' Noting the inquisitive eyes from their three companions, Andy explained, 'It's kind of like a big nightclub. I may have been the entertainment one night.'

Erimem gave the broadest, falsest smile. 'We had no idea you couldn't sing.'

Andy feigned outrage. 'Can't sing? Why, I've hardly ever been so insulted.' She sighed and smiled at Carlisle. 'Be a hero and rescue me from my awful friends by telling up more about the unfortunate Mrs Rollins.'

'I'm afraid there's very little more I can offer,' Carlisle

replied sadly. 'She was quiet when she came aboard and asked for as much privacy as possible.'

'She has my sympathy,' Erimem said, 'both for the loss of her husband and for being forced to endure that loud bore.'

'I think he's sent the couple on the other side of him into a coma,' Helena said, inspecting a grey couple in immaculate but drab clothes. 'I swear he's drained the colour from them.'

'They were like that when they came aboard,' Dorward said. 'I saw them on the quay.'

'They have hardly spoken since they sat down.' Erimem said.

Andy glanced at the grey, middle-aged couple. 'Maybe they just don't have anything more to say to each other? Some couples get that way after a while.'

Erimem shook her head slowly. 'I do not think so. There is rarely affection between those couples. I see great love in the eyes of those people. Especially the woman.'

Ibrahim nudged his many times great aunt. 'Erimem, I do believe you're a romantic at heart.'

'Last week you said I was a student at heart,' she answered, 'and the week before I was a warrior at heart. How many hearts do I have?'

'One very large one,' Helena interjected. 'It's a crawling answer but it gets my husband out of trouble.'

Erimem beamed broadly. 'Thank you.'

'You're right about that couple, though,' Helena mused. 'The...' she looked expectantly to Carlisle.

'The Mitchells,' the officer supplied immediately. 'Mr Mitchell retired recently. He and his wife took this trip to celebrate.'

'And just look at those wild and crazy kids go,' Andy sniffed. 'The party animals.'

'Who is the old man who just sat at the Captain's Table?' asked Nadia.

A balding man of around sixty, impeccably dressed in black tie had greeted Captain Hawkins and the Bischkovas warmly. His greeting for the tweed-dressed young man who arrived a few moments behind him was barely civil.

'Jack Reubens,' said Carlisle. 'He is an industrialist and rather successful.'

42

'But not successful at hiding his dislike for the young fella in tweed,' Ibrahim said.

The young recipient of Reubens' ire took his seat, allowing Carlisle's table a better view of him. 'That is William Hove,' the First Officer said. 'He's rather a well-known free-thinking, radical socialist.'

Andy leaned forward, frowning. 'You say "socialist" like it's a swear word.'

'Or a bad thing,' added Helena.

Carlisle appeared to be bemused by their attitude. 'You're not socialists are you?'

'We don't all knit our own muesli and demand free everything for everybody,' Andy grinned.

'Don't confuse socialism with communism,' Helena said. 'There's a difference between equality of opportunity and equality of outcome. And this probably isn't the place for that kind of discussion.'

A frown appeared on Andy's face. 'Hang about. William Hove? I read some of his stuff for Sociology.'

'Is he a good writer?' Erimem asked.

Andy shook her head. 'Dull, turgid and as bad as you'd imagine a school text book would be.'

Erimem wrinkled her nose in mock sympathy. 'Shame.'

Andy took a sip of her wine. 'There's something about him that sticks in my head for some reason.'

'What is it?' asked Erimem.

Andy shook her head. 'Can't remember. It hasn't stuck all that well in my head.'

Helena snorted in disappointment. 'You're fired.'

'Thanks, doll,' Andy answered, utterly unperturbed as she watched the oldest old ladies she had ever seen shuffle towards the table as if they were imitating Julie Walters in that *Acorn Antiques* thing her Mum has liked so much. 'Oh, he is a rude boy.'

'He didn't stand for those old ladies,' said Nadia Bakshi in surprise.

Carlisle coughed disapprovingly and scowled at the offending Mr Hope. 'No, he didn't. They're the Van Guyser twins, by the way. They're from one of America's oldest

43

families.'

'Really?' Erimem and Helena exchanged a look and laughed at the comment about age.

'Ignore them,' Ibrahim said. 'They're being snobs.'

Andy agreed. 'My friends come from families that can be traced back millennia.'

'We are much older than we look,' Erimem laughed.

'I never comment on a lady's age,' Carlisle said chivalrously. 'The Van Guyser's made their money in shipping and railways.'

'With Noah's Ark and Stevenson's Rocket?' asked Andy.

Helena scowled with feigned outrage. 'Don't be ageist.'

Carlisle continued his 'And there's the final member of the party for the Captain's Table.'

A tall, middle-aged man strode through the Dining Room. He looked at various diners around the brightly lit room with open contempt.

'I do not like this man,' Erimem said flatly.

'Give him a break,' Andy protested. 'He only just got here.' The newcomer snorted with distaste as he pushed past an elderly man. 'No, you're right. He's a git.'

'That's Lord Carston Etheridge,' Carlisle explained. 'He's an industrialist.'

'I remember the name,' Helena nodded. 'As rich as Croesus.'

'And not very popular,' said Nadia Bakshi.

She was right. A harsh laugh came from Etheridge and seemed to fill the room. Countless pairs of eyes glared at the man with animosity, some well veiled, some not so well hidden. Even Carlisle looked at his with disdain.

'Perhaps we should focus on our own meal,' Carlisle suggested.

The dinner continued, with conversation turning to lighter matters. There were occasional moments of difficulty, when the talk moved to subjects which relied solely upon knowledge of the time. Thankfully Helena's memory of living through the time came to their rescue. As wine flowed, the dinner became quite jolly, a mood made far lighter when a small but first class orchestra began playing some tunes of the day. The small dance floor remained empty until the Captain invited a reluctant Olga Bischkova for a rather staid turn around the floor.

Carlisle pushed himself up onto his feet. 'I think I should offer the Captain some moral support.' He gave a brief bow to Helena. 'Doctor Hadmani, would you care to join me?'

'I've got a better idea,' Helena said, rising. 'Why don't I take my incredibly reluctant dancer of a husband for a spin around the floor while you dance with Andy or...'

'Erimem,' Andy said quickly. 'Definitely Erimem.' She smiled cheesily as Carlisle. 'Unless you want to let me lead.'

Carlisle extended a hand towards Erimem. 'Would you care to join me?'

'I will do my best,' Erimem agreed, 'although this is not the style of dance I learned as a child.'

'You've seen Strictly,' Andy grinned. 'Just pretend he's Anton and you'll be fine.'

Erimem proved to be a very quick study, picking up the basic movements of the dance from a few seconds of watching the other couples. 'Clever bugger,' Andy breathed, 'she really has watched Strictly. She's doing heel leads and everything.'

Andy glanced quickly at the remaining two people seated at the table, but Nadia Bakshi and Sergeant Dorward were deep in conversation and had no interest in talking with anyone else. They didn't just have a spark, she thought, they had a full-on fireworks display going on around them.

She turned her attention back to the dance floor which was steadily filling. The businessman Reubens had gallantly invited one of the geriatric Van Geyser twins to dance. At the speed she was moving they'd be in Southampton before she reached the dancefloor. The dullard couple were dancing and Andy saw the connection between them for the first time. It was all in their eyes. Love, affection... and there was fear in there, too. That was interesting. What was Mr Not-so-Dull-Anymore afraid of? The loudmouth soldier had dragged the mousy widow up for a dance where he treated a turn around the dancefloor with the same subtlety as an hour of square bashing on the parade ground.

Others diners Carlisle hadn't got around to talking about yet also filled the floor. It all looked rather nice. Andy wondered how it would look if her girlfriend, Olivia, had been able to join them on this holiday. How would the good people of 1934 have reacted if two young women danced romantically together? *How much of their shit would they lose?* The thought of her girlfriend captaining a privateer ship in the Caribbean more than three centuries in the past brought a smile to Andy's face. Their relationship certainly had challenges but they were making it work. *And Olivia was a phenomenal kisser.* Truth be told, Andy found that she missed Olivia very badly when she wasn't around. She eyed her wine warily. She was thinking serious relationship thoughts and that was usually a sign that she had reached a certain level of tipsy.

The thing with time travelling was that it often put a person off of thinking about their own immediate future. They were just having too much fun in the moment. But what was the future for Andy with Olivia? Was it time for that kind of conversation?

'No!'

The single word, as loud as a scream, snapped Andy back to the present.

Olga Bischkova had abandoned Captain Hawkins and strode towards Carston Etheridge who was leading the reluctant figure of Tatania Bischkova to the dance floor.

Olga caught her daughter's wrist and pulled her away from Etheridge. 'Stay away from her!' she spat at Etheridge.

'What on Earth is the matter?' Etheridge asked, far too calmly. 'It's just a dance.'

He's enjoying this, thought Andy. *He knew this was going to happen and he's enjoying it.*

'You will not go near her,' Olga repeated. 'Never.'

'She's hardly a child,' Etheridge answered. 'She's almost as old as you were when you learned to...' he left just long enough of a pause for the meaning to be evident and vile, '...dance.'

Olga Bischkova's hand cracked against Etheridge's cheek with a sound as harsh as a gunshot.

Instinctively Etheridge's arm pulled back to retaliate, his hand bunched into a fist. He never had the chance to throw the punch.

A small, slight figure caught his wrist and stopped the arm in its tracks.

Etheridge spun to confront his foe. 'What the devil?' he roared at the sight of Erimem easily restraining his arm.

Seeing that the Bischkovas had stepped back out of range,

Erimem pushed Etheridge's hand away.

Etheridge instinctively moved to attack Erimem.

She stared hard into his eyes. 'If you raise your hand against me I will kill you where you stand.'

Etheridge glared back at Erimem for a long moment then turned to the nearest crewman, who happened to be Carlisle. 'Get this darkie out of my way.'

William Carlisle surprised the room and possibly himself by standing his ground against the peer. 'Lord Etheridge, that language is unacceptable.'

Etheridge was startled by First Officer's refusal to simply do as he was told. 'And what are you going to do about it? I'll buy the damn boat just to sack the lot of you.'

'If you do that, then you do that,' Carlisle answered, 'but at the moment I believe you owe this lady an apology.'

'Apologise to one of her kind?' Etheridge snorted in disbelief. 'Never in this life.'

'Meaning?' Andy demanded.

'The ship's full of them,' Etheridge sneered. There was a sheen on his face that usually came with having drunk heavily. He indicated Erimem, Ibrahim and with a flourish, Nadia Bakshi. 'How you can call this First Class when they'll let that kind in I don't know.'

'You'll apologise for that.' Sergeant Dorward had pushed himself up and walked unsteadily across leaning heavily on his stick.

'Got an eye on a dusky maiden, have you?' laughed Etheridge. 'She's out of your league. You haven't got a leg to stand on.' His foot lashed out sharply, kicking Dorward's stick away. The policeman toppled heavily to the floor. Nadia Bakshi hurried to his side.

Etheridge didn't grant the injured man another look. He strode to the door, and spun as he reached for the door. 'I look forward to seeing you all tomorrow. This is going to be a very enjoyable voyage.' He pushed his way through the door and disappeared.

The Dining Room was silent and then became a low buzz of chatter. Captain Hawkins looked utterly lost as questions rained in on him.

Carlisle tried to offer an apology to Erimem but she had already moved to Dorward's side. Helena quickly joined them.

'How does it feel?' Helena asked?

Dorward was already sweating profusely. He answered through gritted teeth. 'Bloody agony. Sorry for swearing.'

'It's all right,' Nadia reassured him.

Helena placed the back of her hand against Dorward's forehead. 'If it helps curse away.' She called to the First Officer. 'Mr Carlisle, where's the ship's surgeon?'

Carlisle pointed across the room. 'Over here. I'll get him.'

Helena's party followed Carlisle's extended finger to the bleary figure still seated at a table. 'That?' Andy demanded. 'He's sozzled.'

Helena made a swift decision. 'I'll examine the sergeant myself. What's closer, his room or the infirmary?'

'His room,' Carlisle replied.

Helena nodded. 'Okay, get a couple of your lads to carry him to his room.'

'No need,' protested Dorward. 'Just get me my stick and I'll get there under my own steam.'

Helena gave the policeman a withering look. 'Are you going to be a good patient or a pain in the arse?'

Dorward didn't wit under the scrutiny. 'What do you think?'

'He is going to be a good patient,' Nadia Bakshi said severely.

'That's you told,' Ibrahim told Dorward.

Andy nudged Helena and headed for the door. 'You'll need your bag. I'll go get it.'

'Thanks, Andy.'

As she held open the Dining Salon doors for the stewards to carry Dorward through, Andy glanced back into the Salon. All she saw were a lot of frightened faces.

'He's asleep,' Helena said. She had shooed her companions along with First Officer Carlisle and Nadia Bakshi out of the room while she examined Dorward's hip. Job done, she allowed them to file back in. 'There's no bone damage. I think he's just bruised and tender.'

'May I see him?' Nadia asked. 'I feel very guilty. This happened to him because he spoke in defence of me.'

Helena stepped aside. 'Help yourself, but I gave him a jab and he's out for the count.'

'I will not disturb him,' Nadia promised.

'What's the prognosis?' asked Carlisle, peering at the sleeping man.

'It may slow his recovery by a few days,' Helena said quietly, 'but I don't think it'll do him any lasting physical harm. In fact, I wouldn't be surprised if it pushed him to work harder to be back at one hundred percent quicker. He's a stubborn sod.'

'And what of the man who did this to him?' Erimem asked Carlisle. There was an edge to her voice that her friends recognised. She was angry, she was outraged and she wanted either justice or revenge.

'Lord Etheridge...' Carlisle's voice faltered. 'I don't know what I can do. He is an incredibly important man.'

'And Sergeant Dorward is not?' Erimem asked bluntly.

Carlisle wilted under the angry gaze. 'You know what money means. There's nothing I can really do to him.'

'I understand it is difficult to stand against power, but you must not let this man treat others in this way.'

Carlisle accepted Erimem's argument. 'I'll talk to the Captain. What happens has to be his decision.'

'I will talk with him also,' Erimem said. She was still obviously angry.

'Let me speak to him first, miss,' Carlisle said in a placating tone. 'It's likely he'll want to talk to you all in the morning. I'll go and see him now.'

Erimem looked set to argue but after looking at the faces of her companions she relented and nodded her assent.

'Goodnight,' Helena said to Carlisle.

The First Officer nodded. 'Goodnight,' he said, slipping out into the corridor.

Helena turned to her three companions. 'You three should get some sleep as well.'

'What about you?' asked Erimem.

Helena shrugged. 'I have a patient. The couch here looks comfy enough.'

Ibrahim looked hard at his wife. 'There is absolutely no chance we're going to talk you out of this, is there?'

Helena's hair bounced as she shook her head. 'Nope.'

Erimem caught Ibrahim's arm and drew him towards the door. 'Then we will leave you in peace.'

'All right,' Helena agreed. She exchanged a quick kiss with Ibrahim. 'Goodnight,' she said before turning to Dorward's other visitor. 'You should get some rest as well, Nadia.'

Nadia nodded absently. 'I will.'

Nope, Helena thought, Nadia was going nowhere. It looked like there might be competition for the couch.

First Officer William Carlisle took the salutes and greetings of the crew he passed. Most of the ship's passengers were now in bed but the crew would be working for a few hours yet.

In truth Carlisle was not looking forward to meeting with Captain Hawkins. His affection for Hawkins was boundless but he knew that the captain would not want to rock the boat by confronting Lord Etheridge. Making an enemy of a rich peer would not be good for either of their careers. Still and all, Etheridge had behaved like a swine and he had attacked an injured and unarmed man. That just wasn't the done thing. With luck the captain would have an idea of what to do. He had sailed for the flag for years. Perhaps he knew someone who could have a word with Etheridge.

Two laughing stewards straightened up sharply as he turned a corner.

'Have you tow got duties to be about?'

'Yes, sir.' The men scuttled off, duly chastised.

Carlisle allowed himself a little smile. Giving the lower ranks a bit of a fright was one of the perks of the job. Plus it kept them on their toes. His smile broadened at the thought of another little perk that kept him on his toes. Daisy Brown. Of course if she thought he had described her as "a perk" she'd have had his guts for garters. No, he told himself, it was the luxury of the out of the way cabin that was the perk. Daisy was... Daisy was rather wonderful. The next time he went home he would take Daisy to meet his mother. It was about time for that, he thought. Daisy would be nervous but his mother would adore her. Mother was a very good sort but she was a worrier. She was concerned that going off to sea would mean that her little boy either never had the chance to meet a nice girl or that he would come back with some mystery woman from exotic climes.

Turning the next corner, Carlisle was so lost in his happy thoughts that it took him a fraction of a second longer than normal to realise what stood in front of him. He managed to open his mouth but he was too slow. No sound ever came. He was hurled against the wall, the back of his skull smashing against the solid wooden panelling, and he dropped to the carpeted floor, his gleaming blue eyes dulled in death.

CHAPTER FOUR

Erimem and Andy had only just slid into their twin beds when the sound of running feet on the deck alerted them that something was wrong. Erimem pulled a silk robe over her period nightgown while Andy hastily tied a dressing gown over her *Ren and Stimpy* pyjamas.

Ibrahim had also been roused by footsteps on his side of the ship, and he hurried into the corridor a few steps behind them.

'What's going on?' he asked.

'No idea,' replied Andy.

Erimem pointed along the corridor. 'They were running in this direction.'

Shouts began to come from the decks. The voices were shocked and frightened. A familiar face peered out of a doorway ahead. 'What the hell's going on?' Helena asked.

'We don't know,' Andy answered. 'We'll find out, though.'

'Buggered if I'm missing out,' Helena muttered. She looked quickly back into Dorward's bedroom. 'Keep an eye on him, would you please, Nadia. Just off to see what the commotion's about.'

While they were relative strangers to the ship, it wasn't difficult to follow the sounds of running and shouting to a decks a few levels down where a crowd of crew had gathered, blocking a corridor.

Erimem grabbed the sleeve of the nearest steward. 'What has happened?'

'I'm not sure, miss,' the steward answered. 'I heard that somebody was dead. An officer.'

The Captain's voice could be heard clearly above the buzz of the crowd. 'Where in the devil is Doctor Griffiths?'

'He was the drunk one?' Erimem asked Helena.

Her friend nodded. 'Paralytic.' She started pushing through the crowd of stewards. 'Let me through. I'm a doctor. Move. Movie it.'

Erimem and Helena pushed through the crowd with Andy and Ibrahim close behind. The staff grumbled but kept their voices low. Even in these situations it didn't do to insult the paying passengers.

'What has happened?' Erimem asked the Captain.

'And how can I help?' Helena added. 'I'm a doctor. I don't think your ship's surgeon will be sober enough to help.'

Captain Hawkins at least had the decency to blush as he offered a limp defence of his surgeon. 'I'm sure he's not that bad.'

Helena refused to accept that. 'I'm sure he is. Now let me see the patient.' She stepped around Hawkins. 'Now who is...' she stopped at the sight of the familiar dace on the ground. 'Ah, shit.'

The others had followed and looked past her to the body. The chorused their dismay at the identity of the dead man.

'Aw shit, no,' Ibrahim breathed.

Andy was equally upset. 'Fuck.'

Erimem's shoulders dropped slightly. 'Damn.'

First Office William Carlisle's dead eyes stared ahead.

Helena didn't wait for permission from Captain Hawkins to kneel by the body. She checked Willima Carlisle's neck and wrist before resting her hand over his heart briefly.

She shook her head. 'I'm sorry. He's gone.'

Erimem knelt by her friend. 'What happened to him?'

'Hard to say.' Helena pressed gently around Carlisle's torso up to his neck. Touching the back of his neck and head, she winced and pulled her hand away. The fingers were sticky and covered with blood. 'The back of his skull is shattered.'

'There's blood and hair on the wall,' Ibrahim said, pointing at a wooden panel.

Andy craned her neck upwards. 'How tall would you say Carlisle was?'

'About six feet,' Ibrahim answered.

Andy reached up, stretching to get her hand up towards the height of the mark on the wall. 'Then how the hell did he get his head up to that height, particularly if he was going backwards?'

'Why would he be going backwards?' Hawkins demanded.

'How else would the back of his head strike the wall?' Erimem answered. She sounded annoyed that she had to explain something so obvious.

'Well, I'm sure we'll work it out, Hawkins said uncertainly. A haunted expression flitted across his face as he looked at the corpse of Carlisle. 'I suppose we should get him out of here and give him some respect.'

'He needs to be properly examined,' Helena agreed, 'but so does the crime scene.'

'Crime scene?' Hawkins paled even further.

'You don't think he did this to himself, do you?' Helena demanded.

'Out of the way. Out of the damned way.' A familiar and unwelcome voice came from behind the stewards who parted quickly. Lord Etheridge pushed the stewards aside even though there was room for him to pass anyway. His valet, Anderson, was close behind and various other passengers weren't far behind. 'What's all the damned noise about?' Etheridge demanded. 'Men running on the decks and shouting. Damned disgraceful racket. Worse than women.'

'I'm sorry for the noise, your Lordship,' Hawkins answered stiffly, 'but one of my officers has been found dead.'

'The First Officer?' That came from Colonel Mackenzie, who had pushed his way to Etheridge's shoulder. 'Damned unfortunate for a man to go that young.'

'Probably drunk,' Etheridge said callously. 'At least that would explain why he spoke to me as he did.'

The man's attitude rankled badly with Andy. 'No, there was another reason he talked back to you,' she snapped. 'It was because you deserved it for being such a dick.'

Etheridge's already flushed face became a little more purple. 'What did you say?'

'You heard,' Andy snapped. 'The man's dead, show him some respect.'

'The girl's hysterical,' Mackenzie said. 'I'll get her out of here.'

'She is not hysterical,' Erimem said sharply, 'and we should all get away from here and let Helena work.'

'Work?' Etheridge said dismissively. 'What do you mean?'

'The lady is a doctor,' Hawkins explained and our own ship's doctor is detained elsewhere.'

Etheridge eyes Helena with a mixture of hunger and disdain. 'Might ask for a physical later myself.'

Ibrahim took a step closer to Etheridge. 'If you ever talk about my wife life that again, you'll need one.'

Etheridge snorted in disgust.

'All right!' Helena snapped. She was angry and made no effort to hide it. 'Everybody out of here. Everybody except a couple of stewards. I'll need them to carry Mr Carlisle to the sickbay.'

'This corridor will need to be closed off until it has been properly examined,' Erimem added.

The idea of actually having something that he knew he could do put some life back into Hawkins. 'All right,' he said, 'everybody leave this corridor. Skinner, you and Bolton stay to help Doctor Hadmani and then rope the corridor off.'

A steward saluted. 'Yes, captain.'

The Captain waved his hands ushering crew and passengers away from the scene. 'Now I suggest you all go back to your beds. We'll deal with this.'

'Bed be damned,' said Etheridge. 'I'll need a drink to get me off to sleep.'

'That's not a bad idea,' Colonel Mackenzie muttered. 'I could do with a stiffener.'

'You know,' Hawkins said to Helena, 'the infirmary on board is usually a busy place. Passengers with *mal-de-mer*, that sort of thing...'

'And a drunk doctor?' Helena's eyebrows rose. 'What are you getting at, Captain?'

Hawkins pointed a finger downwards. 'I was going to suggest that we might put Bill... Mr Carlisle in his own cabin.' A look of horror appeared on his face. 'Oh, dear lord.'

'What is it?'

Hawkins' hand moved to cover his eyes. 'That poor girl.'

'Girl?' Erimem asked. 'What girl?'

Hawkins tilted his head towards his friend. 'Billy's girl. Daisy Brown. She's one of our maids aboard ship.'

'Will she still be awake?' asked Helena.

'She'll be waiting in his cabin,' Hawkins admitted. He moved closer to Helena so that the stewards wouldn't overhear. 'I knew that they were, well... I knew that they were sharing a bed and I told them I'd turn a blind eye to it as long as they were discrete. I saw no harm in it. He wanted to marry the girl and I'm sure she felt the same.'

'So she'll be in bed waiting for him?' Helena asked. Hawkins nodded. 'Well,' Helena said softly, 'that just every kind of shit.' She straightened and glanced at Erimem. 'I assume you overheard all of that?'

'Naturally.'

'Want to come with us?' Helena grimaced. 'I always hated telling people their loved one is dead.'

'I understand. I have spoken to many about losses after battles.' Erimem's hand shot out in front of Hawkins to get his attention. 'However, we must find the identity of the person who did this to Mr Carlisle,' she said quietly. 'We must find them and make them pay for their actions.'

'She means we bring them to justice,' Helena said, more for Erimem's sake than for Hawkins'. 'Not retribution, justice in a court.'

'Of course,' Erimem agreed without a hint of sincerity.

'But how do I find out who did it?' Hawkins asked. He was almost pleading. 'This is a cruise liner. The worst we have happen aboard is minor thefts, and it's Mr Carlisle who usually handles that sort of thing. I'm the manager of a floating hotel. I'm not a trained investigator.'

'Sergeant Dorward is,' Helena said. 'He's a police detective.'

The idea clearly appealed to Hawkins. 'Really? I should speak to him.'

'You can't,' Helena answered. 'He's out cold. I gave him a shot to help him sleep. He won't wake till morning.'

'So what do we do tonight?' Hawkins asked.

'Tell the passengers to lock themselves into their rooms,' Helena said.

Erimem nodded. 'And if they are to be up and moving about the ship, they should be in groups of three. That way if one if the killer, he will always be outnumbered.'

'Yes,' Hawkins muttered, nodding to himself. 'That makes sense. Groups of three. I'll give that instruction.'

Helena indicated for the stewards to lift Carlisle's fallen body. 'We'll get Mr Carlisle to his room first.'

Daisy Brown had fallen apart when informed of Carlisle's death. Hawkins had broken when he tried to tell her, and in the end Helena and Erimem had taken the onerous duty. Daisy had been sedated and put into a spare cabin in a busy corridor so that Carlisle could be laid out on his own bunk.

Helena had performed a preliminary examination on Carlisle. Death had definitely been caused by the back of the sailor's head striking the wall. Opening his shirt she found a large and livid red mark on his chest. Beneath the discoloured skin, the sternum and ribs had shattered.

'There's no resistance when I push on the chest,' she said. 'The impact must have been enormous.'

'His death would have been immediate,' Erimem murmured.

'Yes,' Helena agreed. 'That kind of impact would have damaged the organs as well. He may well have been as good as dead by the time he hit the wall.' She sighed and pulled a sheet over Carlisle's head. 'I'm not going to do a more in-depth examination tonight.'

'Why?'

'Because I've had too much to drink,' Helena answered, 'and so have you. If we're going to investigate this we owe it to Mr Carlisle to be sober when we do it.'

Erimem nodded. 'You are right. We should do this properly. He was a decent man.'

Helena dropped an arm around her friend's shoulders. 'Come on. We'll report to the Captain and then get some sleep.'

Leaving the cabin, Erimem gave instructions to the stewards standing outside. 'Stand guard over him tonight. He deserves that honour. Let no-one in until morning.'

The two women walked off in search of the Captain, leaving

two very uncomfortable stewards standing outside of the cabin door.

The hubbub on ship during the night had roused all of the First Class passengers, and led to intense conversation when they gathered in the Dining Room for breakfast the following morning.

While the passengers gathered to gossip, the crew tending to their needs had the weary look of men and women who had found sleep hard to come by.

Captain Hawkins was circulating around the room offering platitudes and reassurances that there was nothing to worry about. As he left one group and headed for another he was intercepted by Erimem and Andy.

'Good morning, ladies.'

Erimem took the greeting with a slight tilt of her head. 'Last night you asked to be informed when Sergeant Dorward woke up. He is awake now.'

'Helena's giving him another quick check over to see that he hasn't rolled over or hurt himself during the night,' Andy added.

'Thank you.' Hawkins pursed his lips in thought for a moment. 'I should have a word with a couple more passengers then I'll see him in his room.'

'We'll pass that message on,' Andy said.

On the way to the door, Andy saw her friend glaring disdainfully at Lord Etheridge, who was seated alone, eating a hearty breakfast.

'I don't like him either,' Andy said.

Erimem said nothing but led the way out of the Dining Room.

'I'm sorry. I can't do what you want me to do.'

'But you're the only detective aboard, sergeant,' Captain Hawkins protested. 'I need your help.' Away from the passengers and his forced calm, Hawkins looked as if he had aged ten years overnight. There was no doubt that he hadn't slept and the red puffiness around his eyes suggested that he had also shed tears.

Detective Finlay Dorward was seated in a stiff chair by the

cabin's table. To Helena's annoyance he had insisted on not only getting out of bed but also getting dressed.

'I'm in no condition to investigate this murder.' He tapped his sticks. 'It's not just these that slow me. I'm constantly falling asleep.'

'That's your pain medication,' Helena suggested.

Dorward nodded. 'I believe so, but it doesn't matter what the cause it. The outcome is that I can't investigate if I can't stay awake.'

'But you can offer advice,' Erimem suggested.

'Who to?' asked Dorward.

Helena sighed. 'I'll give you three guesses.'

Hawkins returned to the Dining Room in the company of Erimem's party. With them were Nadia Bakshi and Finlay Dorward.

Helena had argued that Dorward should rest but the policeman had refused "to tuck my tail between my legs and hide from that thug".

Using both sticks, Dorward managed to keep up with the rest of the party. He was, however, obviously relieved to slide into a chair when they arrived in the Dining Room. The rest of the group loitered by the table as Hawkins moved to the centre of the room.

'Ladies and gentlemen, if I might have your attention for a moment.' Most of the crowd quietened somewhat but a few continued talking, forcing Hawkins to repeat himself more loudly. 'If I can have your attention please.' The crowd reluctantly fell quiet. 'Thank you,' Hawkins said. 'I'm aware that many of you have heard rumours and stories about what has happened during the night. Unfortunately it's true that our First Officer, Mr Carlisle was found dead in the early hours of the morning.' He held up a hand to halt the chatter and questions. 'Mr Carlisle was a very dear friend...' his voice shook and he took a moment to compose himself. 'We have a police detective among our passengers.' He indicated Dorward. 'Sergeant Dorward will oversee the investigation. I must ask each of you to give any assistance that is asked of you, until we know what happened.'

Etheridge had left his breakfast table. 'Meaning what exactly?' he asked, moving towards them with a sour expression.

Hawkins answered quickly. 'Meaning, your Lordship, that I must ask you to answer Sergeant Dorward's questions.'

Etheridge snorted. 'Not damned likely. He's only a sergeant.'

A rich Scottish voice boomed from behind Etheridge. 'I'm a colonel. I think that's rank enough to ask questions.' The big soldier strode stiffly towards Hawkins. 'Captain, I would be happy to take command of the investigation. Still making use of Sergeant...' he humphed, 'well, the sergeant's skills. But he obviously can't investigate on gammy legs.'

Dorward visibly reddened at his dismissal by the officer.

However, it was Erimem who answered. 'And how can you deal with an investigation when you can't remember the sergeant's name?' she asked.

'Now see here,' Colonel Mackenzie objected, 'I'll not be talked to like that by the likes of her. I'm senior man here. Ranking officer and all that. I'll do the questioning.'

Erimem bristled but didn't have the chance to reply.

'No, Colonel, you will not. Doctor Hadmani and her companions will be assisting *me*,' Dorward told Mackenzie. 'They'll be doing the things I can't. Moving around the ship, examining location, conducting interviews and so on.'

'Well, they won't be interviewing me,' Etheridge said dismissively.

'Or me,' said Mackenzie. 'I've never heard such a ridiculous idea.'

'Why is it ridiculous?' Erimem asked.

'It's obvious,' Mackenzie blustered. 'Anyone can tell she can't ask a gentleman questions.'

Erimem's eyes narrowed. 'Why is that?'

'It's obvious,' Mackenzie snapped.

'What you're trying to say without actually using the words is that she's not white,' Helena said sourly.

Mackenzie's nostrils flared in anger. 'I'd say that was equally obvious, wouldn't you?'

'And she's female,' Helena persisted, 'so she's clearly useless.'

'You're twisting my words.'

Helena snorted. 'You're very lucky my friend is in a good mood or she might just twist your neck, Colonel, and I do assure you, she could do it with ease and without a second thought. Whatever your training may be, I promise you on a stack of Bibles, her training is better.'

The challenge to his army training cut Mackenzie deeply. 'Poppycock. Sit down and...'

'No, Colonel, you sit down,' Dorward barked sharply. 'I am in charge of the investigation into this murder. You may be army but you are also a suspect.'

'Damn your impudence, I object to that,' Mackenzie roared.

Erimem stepped protectively between Mackenzie and Dorward. 'Object as much as you wish, but you were observed in a loud disagreement with the one who is dead. You had anger in you for him.' She took a step closer to the soldier. He towered over her but she showed no sign of being intimidated. 'You will sit or I will sit you down.'

'Who the Devil do you think you are?' Mackenzie hissed.

'Military Intelligence,' Andy said. All eyes turned to her in surprise, even those of her own companions. 'We weren't supposed to break cover till we get back to England but we're aboard ship now and we won't see shore till Southampton, so there's no harm in telling you all. We're Military Intelligence.'

Mackenzie looked at the unlikely party with open disbelief. 'I assume you have proof of that?' he challenged,

'Our identification is all safely hidden in my quarters,' Andy replied. 'I'll go and collect it, while my colleagues begin their work.'

'Go with her, Ibrahim,' Erimem said softly. 'There is a killer here. We should take care.'

Ibrahim nodded and followed Andy from the room.

'Captain,' Erimem said, turning to the captain, 'the Colonel said you would wish for the military to take on this investigation. I assume that you are agreeable to Military Intelligence taking this role and assisting Sergeant Dorward?'

'Well,' the captain said uneasily, 'I would say yes obviously, though, you're, well...'

'Women?' Helena offered, 'and of colour?' She shook her

head. 'Not you as well, Captain! I would strongly advise you to forget your preconceptions about either gender or race. It will let us get on with our work much more quickly and it will irritate us a good deal less.'

'I am particularly easily irritated,' Erimem added menacingly.

'I believe you,' the captain said, eyeing Erimem nervously.

The door opened and Ibrahim followed Andy into the room.

'You were quick,' Helena said.

Andy's eyebrow lifted. 'Were we? We hurried.' She handed a sheaf of papers across to the captain. 'I think you'll find these in order.'

The captain skimmed through the various documents, his face a mixture of relief and surprise. 'They do seem to be fine to me.'

'Let me see.' Colonel snatched the papers from the captain, eager to show them up as forgeries. He was quickly disappointed. 'Definitely genuine,' he said after inspecting them briefly. He handed the papers back to the captain who relayed them back to Andy. 'So,' Mackenzie went on, 'you're in charge, are you?' His question was aimed at Dorward but it was Andy who answered.

'We are,' she said. 'Well, Sergeant Dorward is, but we'll be helping out.'

Mackenzie straightened his back further and rocked back on his heels. 'And what do you plan to do?'

Dorward replied immediately. 'We're going to talk to everyone in First Class to see if they heard anything and to identify their whereabouts when Mr Carlisle was killed.'

Etheridge sighed as if the whole thing was the most frightful bore. 'Why only First Class?' he asked. 'Isn't it more likely that this is the work of the lower class passengers?'

'There is no way for anyone from lower decks to reach the scene of the crime,' Erimem answered. 'It was someone in this First Class area of the ship.'

'Outrageous!' snapped Mackenzie.

Dorward pushed himself up on his sticks. 'But true, nonetheless. We will be talking to everyone in First Class.'

Erimem spoke to Captain Hawkins. 'Do you have a room we

can use for these interrogations?'

'Interviews,' Helena corrected softly. 'Interviews, not interrogations.'

Erimem raised a delicate eyebrow. 'Yes,' she conceded with no sincerity. 'Interviews. Probably.'

Hawkins indicated a side door. 'There's a small private room through here, a private dining saloon. In case select passengers should care for a private party.'

Andy and Erimem crossed to the door and looked inside. A rather charming compact room with just two tables, comfortable chairs and a pair of splendid couches waited silently.

'Looks perfect,' said Andy.

Erimem nodded. 'It would be difficult for anyone to escape from.'

They returned to Hawkins.

'It's perfect for what we need,' Andy said.

'Good,' said Dorward. 'We'll move in there and get started. We'll need paper to take notes.'

I learned shorthand,' Nadia Bakshi offered tentatively.

'Are you good at it?' Dorward asked.

'I think so.'

Andy was impressed. 'None of us can do it so I'd say you got the job.' She looked at Dorward. 'Sergeant?'

Erimem offered her support for the idea. 'It makes sense.'

Dorward conceded to the sense in the notion. 'Agreed,' he said to Nadia, 'you can take the notes. My handwriting looks like shorthand but it's just awful handwriting.' He turned to his new deputies. 'We might as well have the Colonel first.'

'No,' Erimem interjected. 'Make him wait. He is angry. If he has something to hide, being forced to wait will only make him angrier.'

A wolfish smile crept onto Dorward's face. 'That's fair. He can stew a while.'

Erimem continued, 'The other one. Lord Leatherbridge.'

'Etheridge,' Andy corrected. 'Leatherbridge is the surgery in *Doctors.*'

Erimem's nose wrinkled. 'Yes,' she accepted, 'Etheridge. He does not want to speak, so he should be picked first – but we must make it look random. He is not being chosen as a mark of respect.'

'I don't think anybody here has much respect for him,' Dorward muttered.

'Listen,' Helena said, 'this process doesn't need all of us.'

'Meaning?' Andy asked.

Helena vaguely waved a finger towards the door. 'Meaning I should go and perform a full examination on Mr Carlisle.'

The idea met with Erimem's approval. 'And I very much wish to see the place where he was killed. But I also want to be here for these interrogations. I've read Sherlock Holmes.'

Erimem looked to Dorward for agreement. 'You have no objection, sergeant?'

Dorward gave a wry smile. 'I get the feeling I'm only a passenger here but I'm happy for Miss Hansen...'

Andy interrupted to amen him. 'Andy.'

'Not if I'm on duty,' Dorward said. 'I'm happy for Miss Hansen to study the scene.'

Andy gave a slight bow. 'I shall happily be your stand-in Sherlock.'

Erimem turned to her many times great nephew. 'Ibrahim, would you go with her?'

Helena nudged her husband towards Andy. 'Better if you do. You know you're not good with blood. If I do any kind of post mortem...'

'Okay,' Ibrahim agreed quickly, 'I'll be with Andy.'

Erimem pushed the door open. 'Good. There is somewhere else I would like you to look too.'

CHAPTER FIVE

While the rest of the party set off to begin their investigations, Erimem returned to the Dining Room and looked around the gathered passengers. None of them looked at all comfortable. Even the Captain was on edge.

Colonel Mackenzie straightened his back and squared his shoulders. 'If we must have this charade, I'll go first.'

Erimem let him take a couple of steps before stepping to the side to block his path. 'Not so fast. We will be talking to someone else first.' She looked around nonchalantly. Some of the passengers wilted under her gaze. Even Captain Hawkins looked uneasy. He had fallen several steps in her estimation with his casual sexism and misogyny. She didn't care if he was just a product of his time. For a moment she mulled calling him first but there was something in the utterly disinterested and dismissive manner of Etheridge that rankled her. She also had the feeling that they would get most from this man by interrogating him when he most did not want to talk with them.

'We will talk to you first,' she said to Etheridge. 'You have had plenty to say so far.'

Etheridge didn't move. 'I have no intention of taking part in this farce.'

Part of Erimem had hoped Etheridge would refuse to co-operate. 'Your choice is either walk through or we put you in handcuffs and drag you through.'

There was anger in Etheridge's reply, but also a hint of fear that she might carry out her threat. 'You wouldn't dare. I would end your career.'

Erimem held her ground. 'Better men than you have tried. I am here. They are not.' She pointed at the door to the private Dining Saloon. 'Through here.'

Lord Etheridge reluctantly made his way into the small saloon. His manner made it clear that this interview was an affront and quite beneath him.

Dorward was seated at one of the tables, with Nadia at his side taking notes. A single chair sat on the other side of the table.

Dorward didn't rise to greet Etheridge. 'Sit down, please.'

'I don't need permission to sit,' Etheridge bristled.

'It was not a request,' Erimem said from behind him.

'Please sit down,' Dorward repeated coldly.

Etheridge sat but couldn't resist making another threat. 'You can all be damned sure I'll be talking with your superiors when I get back to London.'

Dorward looked thoroughly disinterested. 'I'm sure you will. Tell me, why are you on board the *Agamemnon*?'

Etheridge snorted in disgust. 'Is that the best you can come up with? Why am I aboard? I'm going home, you imbecile.'

Dorward ignored the insult. 'Where were you before boarding?'

'Alexandria of course.'

'Anywhere else?' Dorward asked patiently.

Etheridge sighed in irritation. 'Of course. I had a little tour of various spots around the Mediterranean, trying the foods, the wines...' his eyes shifted lewdly from Nadia to Erimem, '...trying some of the local delights. You know how it is.'

Dorward ignored the innuendo. 'I'll need a copy of your travel itinerary.'

'You'll have to see my man Anderson for that,' Etheridge said. 'I don't have anything of the like myself.'

'Naturally,' said Erimem, moving around behind him to stand by the table. 'Other than trying... local culture, what was the purpose of your trip?'

The peer looked at her as if she was a simpleton. 'A holiday, what do you think?'

'I don't know,' Erimem answered. 'That is why I am asking.'

'It's damned difficult running businesses and sitting in the Lords. I deserve a break.'

'What kind of businesses do you operate?' Erimem asked.

Her ignorance seemed to offend Etheridge. 'Are you serious?'

Erimem remained impassive. 'Very much so.'

'As *everybody* who is anybody knows,' Etheridge said, 'I have a diverse and successful portfolio covering everything from housing to engineering.'

Erimem ignored the boast. 'Could you be more specific please?'

His inability to threaten or frighten these people irked Etheridge. 'I could but I don't see why I should.'

Dorward tapped a pen irritably in the table. 'Because this is a murder investigation and we are both asking.'

'Very well,' Etheridge finally conceded. 'If it gets this sham over with sooner. I own and rent out hundreds of houses in London and in several other cities. I have extensive farming interests in England and around the Empire and I run rather a lot of factories.'

'What do the factories make?' Erimem asked.

'A range of things from large to small. I could have Anderson do you a list of those too.'

Dorward nodded. 'That would be appreciated. As I recall, you made a good deal of your fortune during the Great War.'

'I did my duty,' Etheridge said with a sham of pride, 'suppling my country with weapons and munitions.'

'Without cost?' asked Erimem.

Etheridge just snorted.

Dorward nudged Nadia's arm. 'We can take that as a no.'

'I would be no use to the country if I bankrupted myself. I kept prices low because I'm a patriot.'

'I'm sure you are,' Dorward didn't try to sound as if he believed the peer. 'Do you operate a shipping line?'

'Of course not. Why?'

'Well, we heard you threatening to buy this ship so you could sack Mr Carlisle.'

'I said I don't own a liner. I didn't say whether I would seriously buy one or not.'

That didn't tally with how Erimem remembered events. She logged that but chose not to confront it yet. 'So you were just threatening Mr Carlisle?'

'More than likely.'

'Why would you do that?' asked Dorward.

'I didn't like his tone.'

'You don't like my tone either,' said Erimem. 'My skin tone.'

Etheridge's lip curled in a sneer. 'Clever word play. You must feel so clever.'

'Perhaps.'

'You threatened Mr Carlisle,' Dorward said. 'Because you didn't like his tone?'

'I threatened him because I could,' Etheridge said simply, 'and because I knew there was nothing he could do about it. I threatened him because it would humiliate him or because I would have the chance to destroy his prospects later.'

'You can't do that now,' Dorward said mildly.

'It's damned disappointing.'

'Did you know Mr Carlisle before you boarded the *Agamemnon*?' asked Erimem.

'Of course not,' Etheridge sneered. 'He's hardly in my set.'

Dorward made a show of looking at some papers. 'The *Agamemnon* is hardly where we would expect to find someone as wealthy as you. Is your business going well? Are you in financial difficulties and chose a cheaper holiday?'

The insult clearly hit its mark. 'Don't be impertinent!' Etheridge snapped. 'My businesses are in rude health. Not that it's any of your business.'

Dorward set the papers down and stared very intently at Etheridge. 'At the moment it is up to me to decide what is and isn't my business, and your business is very much my business.'

'What do you think of people of colour?' Erimem asked suddenly. 'In particular, what do you think of strong women of colour?'

Etheridge didn't answer the question. 'What has that got to do with anything?' he snapped.

Erimem replied, 'It would tell us much about you.'

The idea of being judged by lesser members of society clearly rankled Etheridge. 'I think everyone has a place in life and they should stick to that. And to their own kind.'

'Really?' Erimem said coldly.

'Yes, *really*. The War gave people ideas above their station. We need to reset the boundaries between classes. And races.'

'And sexes?' Dorward asked mildly.

'Of course.'

Dorward continued to press Etheridge. 'It seems that Countess Bischkova would agree. She didn't want you anywhere near her daughter.'

'Really?'

Dorward's gaze didn't waver from Etheridge. 'Why do you think that was?'

'She's highly strung,' Etheridge said dismissively. 'You know what these foreigners are like.'

Erimem made a show of shrugging. 'Being a foreigner myself I don't know.'

Dorward continued the questioning. 'Why was she so against you dancing with her daughter?'

'Ask her.'

'We intend to,' Erimem said quickly. 'You first.'

'Why was she so against you dancing with the girl?' Dorward repeated. 'Do you know her? Have you met her before you came onto this ship?'

The irritation in Etheridge's voice grew. 'I meet a lot of people through the Lords and my business. I imagine that she met with a number of men through her business.'

'And what business is that?' asked Dorward.

'Entertainment. She owned a club.'

Dorward continued, 'And you met her there?'

'Possibly.'

'She's a beautiful woman,' said Dorward. 'Are you likely to forget meeting a woman who looks like that?'

'I am fortunate to meet many beautiful women.' Entitlement oozed from Etheridge.

'Do *they* consider themselves fortunate?' Erimem asked coolly.

'Damned cheek.' Etheridge snapped.

That had hit a nerve. Dorward leaned forward. 'It's a fair question.'

Etheridge reached for bluster and outrage. 'It's impertinent, as is this entire ridiculous charade.'

Erimem walked behind Etheridge, deliberately bumping into the back of his chair to disquiet him. 'You are very defensive. Do you have something to hide?'

'I don't answer to a foreigner or to a mere sergeant.'

Erimem wasn't cowed by the harsh tone of his answer. 'You will answer or I will make you answer.'

'If we assume that you did know Countess Bischkova,' Dorward said, pulling Etheridge's thoughts in another direction, 'isn't it a coincidence that you should meet her on this ship?'

'If you say so,' Etheridge sniffed.

'How many times have you met her?' asked Dorward.

'I really can't say.'

'Can't or won't?'

'Do you know anyone else on board the ship?' Erimem added.

'Anderson, my valet.'

'Other than him?' Dorward asked, controlling his impatience.

Etheridge gave a condescending laugh. 'They're not really my set.'

Erimem snapped, 'And that is not an answer to his question.'

'It's the only answer you're getting.'

Erimem nudged Etheridge's chair again. 'You are being deliberately unhelpful.'

'And you should remember that you're talking to a peer of the realm and one of the wealthiest men in the Empire.'

Erimem snorted. 'That does not impress me. You do not impress me.'

Etheridge looked at her – actually really looked at her – for the first time. 'I don't, do I?'

Erimem's back straightened with pride as it always did when she talked of her father. 'My father was a king and a great warrior. I am not impressed by you.'

'Some jungle chief?' Etheridge sneered. 'Friend of Tarzan?'

Erimem gave a cold smile. 'I understand that cultural reference. I met Johnny Weissmuller at a party in Hollywood. He was very tall and very polite.'

'How exciting for him.'

'Do you know anyone else on board this ship?' Dorward

asked suddenly.

'I already answered that,' Etheridge answered angrily.

'No, you didn't,' Dorward replied coolly.

Etheridge sighed elaborately. 'Are we nearly finished, *constable*?'

'Are you likely to answer any of our questions clearly?' Dorward snapped at Etheridge.

'This is not a ship of the highest calibre,' Erimem said.

'So?'

Erimem continued, 'Why would someone like you, someone impressed with your own status, travel on a ship that is not of the highest standard available. There were better ships sailing similar routes leaving tomorrow and two days ago. Why choose this one?'

'It suited my needs.' Etheridge answered.

'Which are?' Dorward pressed.

'My affair.'

'That's not an acceptable answer,' said Dorward.

Etheridge shrugged. 'That's not my problem.'

'This is a waste of time,' Erimem snapped angrily. 'We should torture him so that he gives us answers.'

'She's joking,' Dorward said quickly. 'You are joking, aren't you?' he asked Erimem.

Erimem humphed. 'Probably. There is little to be gained if *this* will not answer our questions.'

'I agree,' Dorward said, carefully not addressing Etheridge directly until he had to. 'You can go, but we will want to talk to you again later.'

'And we will be going through your cabin,' Erimem added.

Etheridge snapped to his feet. 'You certainly will not!'

Erimem glanced at her wristwatch. 'I think you may find we already are.'

'Finish your breakfast,' Dorward said. 'Our examination will be complete by the time you finish.'

Etheridge's nostrils flared in anger. 'I shall be complaining to the Home Secretary about this. I shall finish both of your careers.'

'I'm sure you will,' Dorward said. 'You may go.' Etheridge spun and stomped from the room. 'What a delightful man,'

Dorward sniffed.

Nadia placed her pen down. 'You both taunted him and antagonised him deliberately.'

'Yes,' Erimem answered.

'Why?'

Erimem shrugged. 'Because we do not like him?'

'I shouldn't agree to that,' Dorward said quickly.

'And because people make mistakes when they are emotional,' Erimem added. 'Helena showed that with the German lunatic last night.'

'True,' Dorward said. 'Who is next on the list?'

Nadia checked her paperwork. 'The German lunatic.'

Dorward sighed. 'That should be fun.'

Ship's doctor Peter Griffiths had not reacted well to finding himself usurped as the primary medic aboard the *Agamemnon*. He had argued with Helena to no avail.

'I'll have you know I am the ship's surgeon aboard.'

Helena had waved him away. 'And I can have you arrested if you get in my way. Game, set and match to me.' She had relented somewhat as she remembered that the dead officer was a shipmate and possibly a friend of Griffiths. 'However, if you would care to assist me I would always be appreciative of hearing a colleague's opinion.'

That had calmed Griffiths somewhat, though Helena began to regret including him as they stood together in Carlisle's cabin, looking down at the dead man. Griffiths stank of stale sweat and booze. His dilated pupils suggested that he was still carrying a healthy belt of alcohol in his system.

'Did you know Mr Carlisle well?' she asked Griffiths.

The ship's doctor nodded stiffly. 'Reasonably so. I doubt if you would say we were close friends. We were different generations, and he was First Officer and my superior, so no, I wouldn't say that we were good friends. Good shipmates, I think. I liked and respected him. I think he felt the same about me.'

That sounded just stiff upper lipped enough to be true. 'Fair enough,' Helena accepted. 'Tell me, is there somewhere cold on board ship?'

'Why?'

Helena cast a wave at the portholes. 'The sun's not been up for long but this room is getting warm. I think we should keep him somewhere cold and probably conduct the examination there as well.'

'Of course.' Griffiths thought for a moment. 'There are a couple of storage rooms below decks which never warm up. We set them aside for cold cargo. At least one is empty on this voyage.'

Helena nodded. 'Good. We'll have Mr Carlisle moved down there.'

Andy and Ibrahim had returned to the scene of the murder – or *CSI Agamemnon* as Andy had dubbed it.

'Too soon?' she asked, seeing Ibrahim grimace. 'Bad taste?'

'Just a bit,' Ibrahim nodded.

Andy grimaced. 'That's the weird thing about time travel. The poor man died last night, but he also died eighty five years ago.'

Ibrahim agreed quickly. 'I know. It's a very odd sensation.'

'I shouldn't have been so glib,' Andy castigated herself. 'He was a decent sort of bloke.'

'Then let's see if we can find out what happened to him.'

Andy nodded resolutely. Doing something positive would ease the pangs of guilt from her thoughts. 'I just have a big gob sometimes. I quite liked Carlisle. He was stuffy and old fashioned...'

'Because he was from this time period.'

Andy gave a slow, sad bob of her head. 'He stood up to Lord Moneybags, though. That took guts.'

Ibrahim looked at the bloodstain high on the wall. 'Do you think His Lordship could have lifted Carlisle up to that height?'

Andy looked up at the mark and sucked her bottom lip thoughtfully. 'How tall are you?'

Ibrahim shrugged. 'A bit under six feet?'

'A big bit.' Andy's eyebrows raised. 'And how tall are you really?'

'About five foot ten,' Ibrahim admitted.

Andy thought quickly. 'And that mark is about two feet above your head. So, it's like we thought last night, it's eight feet up.'

'I'd say so,' Ibrahim agreed. 'The seas were calm last night, so there was no rocking or anything like that.'

'So we still don't know how the hell he got up there.'

Andy's hair flashed as she shook her head. 'I haven't got a Scooby. Do you think Lord Scumbag could have lifted him up that high?'

Ibrahim snorted. 'Not a chance. What about the soldier, though? Colonel Blimp?'

'He's a big lad,' Andy conceded, 'and he'll be well trained.'

'Carlisle was a solid six feet, though,' Ibrahim countered. 'He's have to have been taken by surprise.'

'And lifted two feet?' Andy murmured. 'It's not exactly likely, is it?'

Ibrahim sighed. 'Not really.' He peered again at the bloody stain on the wall. 'He must have hit that wall with a hell of a force.'

'At least it would have been quick,' Andy agreed. She loomed at the opposing wall. 'This is a narrow corridor, right?'

'Right.'

'There aren't any scuff marks on the wall or the...' her voice tailed off. 'Wait a minute.'

'What is it?'

Andy dropped to a knee and pointed at a small gouge in the wooden floor. 'Something dug into that floor.'

Ibrahim rapped his knuckles on the floor. 'This is hard wood. Whatever did that had some serious power behind it.' He frowned. 'Some kind of machine.'

'Let's see.' Andy had pulled a pen from her pocket and poked it into the gouge mark. After working at the floor for a second a small fragment if something hard and white skidded across the floor and hit against the wall. Andy picked it up and peered at it.

'What is it?' Ibrahim asked.

Andy handed the object across. 'We need to see Helena.'

The body of First Officer Carlisle had been moved to a cold

cargo hold in the belly of the *Agamemnon*. It was a large rectangle, nothing more than a metal box in the bowels of the ship. It was cold and it was dank, with a sense of damp even though Helena knew the ship was sound. It was probably only in her mind. She knew that they were below the waterline. She pushed all of that aside and returned her attention to the body lying on a table underneath the strong lights that glared overhead.

'I'll show you what we found,' Helena said to Andy and Ibrahim, who were standing a good way back from the body. 'Don't worry,' she added, 'we didn't do a full post mortem on him.'

'Thank God for that,' Ibrahim muttered. He and Andy moved forward.

'Why didn't you give him the works?' Andy asked.

Helena lightly brushed a stray strand of hair away from Carlisle's forehead. 'We don't have permission. Besides, there's no need.' She pointed first at the back of Carlisle's head. 'The back of his skull – the Occipital Bone to be precise was shattered by the impact with the wall.'

'And that's what killed him?' Andy asked.

Helena's grimace suggested it was more complex than that. She lifted the white cloth she had placed over the dead man's chest. A small incision had been made into his chest but that was dwarfed by the huge bruise on his chest. It was centred with a large central discolouration on the sternum and five long thick tendrils creeping out from that central bruise in an unmistakable shape.

'That looks like a hand,' Ibrahim said slowly.

Andy shook her head. 'It can't be. She placed her own hand over the chest. The mark dwarfed her splayed hand. 'My hands aren't big but this must have been huge.'

'And powerful,' Helena agreed. Using tweezers she lifted a segment of bone from a small metal dish. 'I took this from inside his chest.' As she lifted the bone it broke into three or four pieces and dropped back into the dish. 'I didn't have to cut it loose. His sternum and ribs were shattered by a huge impact. Fractures run all the way through the bone. It was almost pulverised.' She carefully began replacing the cloth over Carlisle's chest, hiding the wound, but Andy caught her hand.

'We should photograph this to show Erimem and Dorward,' said Andy.

Helena nodded. 'You're right. 'Got your phone?'

'Yep.' Andy produced her Samsung Galaxy and took half a dozen pictures of Carlisle's chest.

'What the hell is that?' Doctor Griffiths asked, looking at the slim device in bemusement.

Andy looked at him almost in surprise. She had all but forgotten the ship's surgeon was there. 'New bit of kit,' she said. 'Miniature camera. It does a few other things as well. I'm afraid it's classified at the moment.'

'Best if you forget you ever saw it,' Helena suggested.

Griffiths nodded his agreement. 'I wish I could forget this whole voyage.'

Ibrahim indicated the hand shaped bruise as Helena covered it. 'Could he have survived that injury?'

Helena shook her head. 'I very much doubt it. I'd guess he was probably as good as dead by the time he hit the wall.' She sighed. 'We should tell Erimem and Dorward what we found.'

'Found!' the word shouted in Andy's mind. She plucked from her pocket the small object she had dug from the floor. 'We found this at the murder scene,' she said, handing it across to Helena. 'I could be completely wrong but that looks like...'

'A fingernail of some sort?' Helena said, squinting at the small fragment. 'Or maybe a claw? It's not like anything I recognise.'

Griffiths moved closer and tried to look at the fragment in Helena's hand. 'Are you saying an animal killed Mr Carlisle?' he demanded. The ship creaked as it had done countless times since they had entered the room. This time Griffiths looked terrified. 'Are you suggesting there's a wild animal on this ship?'

'We're not suggesting anything,' Andy said.

'Andy's right,' Helena agreed, 'we don't have enough data to suggest anything yet.'

Griffiths ignored her. 'What kind of animal could do this to a man?' His voice was rising, becoming hysterical. 'A bear? A gorilla, maybe?'

'Why would there be a gorilla on board?' Andy asked calmly.

'There's a market for them,' Griffiths answered. 'The gentry and the nobs, they like to import or even smuggle exotic animals to keep as pets on their estates. It's a sign of prestige.'

'That's true at this time,' Helena confirmed quietly.

Ibrahim had picked up on something else the ship's surgeon had said. 'You said "smuggle", didn't you? Does this ship smuggle live animals back to England?'

Griffiths paled. 'I...' his voice choked dryly. 'I don't know.'

'Oh, Dr Griffiths,' Helena said slowly, 'you really are a very bad liar.'

'I'm not lying!' came the automatic reply.

Andy's nose twitched in a sniff. 'I definitely catch the whiff of burning Y-fronts, don't you?' She turned to Griffiths. 'Liar, liar, pants on fire.'

Helena carefully put the claw into her pocket. 'Doctor Griffiths, I think it's time you had a chat with Sergeant Dorward.

Chapter Six

Junior Lieutenant Arthur Mills was, at least technically, in command of the *Agamemnon*. He had been going about his duties, looking after the Second Class passengers when he had been summoned by the captain and told that Mr Carlisle was indisposed and that Mills had to step up and take his place. With Captain Hawkins stuck in First Class doing whatever it was they were all doing in there – that entire section of the ship was out of bounds to everyone – Mills was in command. And he wasn't enjoying it much. At just twenty four he was far younger than any of the other men serving on the ship. He was inexperienced and they all knew it. They were watching him, waiting for him to make a mistake or fall flat on his face. Admittedly, some of them had already seen him do that on his first week aboard when he had slipped on a freshly polished deck. None of them would have laughed at Mr Carlisle. They all respected Mr Carlisle and they liked him, too. They had backed off from the maid Daisy Brown when it became obvious that she had set her cap for the First Officer. She was wasting her time, of course. Mr Carlisle was prohibited from romantic entanglements with other members of the crew. He was a gentleman and he was an officer. He would never break that rule.

The crew were slouching. They would never have slouched if Captain Hawkins was there.

'How's our heading?' Mills barked suddenly. That made Bullman jump, he though with satisfaction.

'On course, Lieutenant,' the sailor answered. 'Speed as ordered.'

'Good,' Mills said briskly. 'Make sure it stays that way, and straighten up the lot of you. You're not relaxing on deck.'

Mills could feel the hate in the glares the crew only just hid from him. He didn't care. He had showed them who was in charge.

As he turned away to look into the distance, Mills was unaware that there was something much worse than hate aimed at him by his crew.

Some were simply laughing silently at him.

'Did you find anything in the ignorant Lord's rooms?'

Helena shook her head. 'We haven't searched them yet.'

An irritated frown puckered Erimem's brow. 'Why not?'

Helena refused to back down to her friend's annoyance. 'Don't go all Pharaoh on us. We've all been busy and we've got a few things we thought you all should know.'

Erimem scowled for a moment before letting it slide. 'I am sorry,' she said in a contrite tone. 'It is just that I sense that there is something wrong with that man.'

'He's an arsehole?' suggested Andy.

'Oh.' Nadia Bakshi looked at Andy with shock.

Andy winced. 'Sorry. I forgot we had company. My apologies, Nadia. I didn't mean to offend you.'

'It's fine,' Nadia answered. 'Really. I'm sure I must have heard worse.' She didn't sound particularly convincing. A wicked gleam appeared on her face. 'Besides, I think you are right. He really is an arsehole.' She glanced at Dorward. 'I'm sorry. That was very rude of me.'

Dorward laughed. 'I'm in the police. The polis as we say. Believe me, anybody in the polis in Edinburgh has heard worse.' He smiled. 'And said worse.'

The couple's interaction had no interest for Erimem just at

that moment. 'What did you find?' she asked Helena.

'We'll start with the examination of Carlisle,' Helena answered. 'Andy, could you call up the pictures?'

'No worries.' Andy produced her phone and swiped the screens. 'With you in a sec,' she said as Erimem and Helena both moved closer. She swiped the screen. 'They're in the camera folder.' She yelped. 'Not those! You never saw those.' She swiped quickly through a very different set of pictures until she found the photographs she had taken minutes earlier in the empty hold. 'Well, that was embarrassing.'

Ibrahim shook his head. 'Not asking.'

'Best not to, dear,' Helena said, before adding to Andy, 'and you might want to switch those to a different folder. "For Olivia's Eyes Only" or something?'

'You don't say.' Andy tilted her phone so that the picture filled the entire screen. She set the phone down on the table. 'There. '

Dorward leaned closer and stared in shock. 'What the devil is this?'

'No time for that,' Helena said brikly. 'It's just a new bit of equipment that takes, stores and displays photographs.'

Dorward was still shocked. 'In colour?'

'Obviously,' Helena answered. 'Now this is Mr Carlisle. We have him downstairs in the coldest hold on the ship. When I examined him I found that the back of his skull was crushed, but as you see there was a huge bruise on his chest. Andy,' can you show us a close up?'

Andy carefully swiped to the next photograph and zoomed in on the bruised chest. 'There you go.'

'A hand,' Erimem said flatly. Her eyes narrowed. 'How big is that hand?'

Andy swiped through to the next picture. 'I knew you'd ask so I took one with my hand beside it for reference.'

'It is enormous,' Erimem said slowly.

'And it crushed Carlisle's chest when it hit him,' Helena said. 'The bones shattered. Near as damn it pulverised the sternum.'

Dorward looked at his own hand. 'I've got a fair sized paw but that thing's at least twice the size of mine.' He looked around the group. 'Have any of you ever seen a man with hands that size?'

'Well,' Helena said with a humourless smile, 'the ship's doctor mentioned something about smuggling animals back to Blighty for toffs to keep as pets.'

'You think an animal did this?' Dorward sounded unconvinced.

'We don't know,' Helena admitted before placing the fragment Andy had found onto the table. 'But Andy found this embedded in a hard wood floor. It's claw or a nail... and I'm sure it's not from a human.'

Dorward visibly paled under his suntan. 'So we have a wild animal on board?'

'We don't know,' Helena admitted, 'but something killed Mr Carlisle by slamming him one handed against a wall.'

'Apes are the only other animals with hands like that, aren't they?' mused Dorward. 'Are you suggesting we've got King Kong running wild on the boat?'

'I was going to say Grodd,' Andy shrugged, 'but it makes sense.'

'Does it?' Erimem asked. 'Where would a gorilla hide on a ship such as this?'

'You haven't been down to the guts of this ship,' Helena said. 'It's a rabbit warren of passages and corridors.'

Erimem shook her head. 'But surely someone would have seen it?'

'Maybe somebody did,' Dorward said quietly, 'and that was what got him killed.'

Erimem was obviously unconvinced but she didn't argue any further. 'We will have to search the ship.'

Helena raised a hand to slow things. 'I'd suggest we talk to the captain first. The ship's doctor hinted that if anything shady was going on the captain would have to know.'

'All right,' Dorward agreed, 'let's talk to Captain Hawkins.'

Daisy Brown was lost.

Not physically, of course. She knew her way around the Agamemnon as well as anyone but emotionally she was utterly lost.

William Carlisle had been everything to her. He had been kind and funny and he had been a gentleman. She had fallen for him almost in the first moment she had seen him while the ship was still in port at Southampton. He had resisted the idea of them becoming involved in a relationship for a long time and even when they had begun stepping out it had taken her weeks to seduce him into her bed. Of course, he had thought it was all his doing, but Daisy had been careful to make sure he would think that. She let him think he was in charge, but in truth, she was easing him towards the altar. There was nothing malicious or underhand in her actions. She had been in love with the man, and she saw that same emotion reflected in his eyes. She had simply been helping him to push their relationship where they both wanted it to go.

Daisy found herself in the doorway of the cold cargo hold where William Carlisle had been taken for examination. The bright light blazed above him as he lay still on a table. Every step closer was difficult, as if she had to fight to force herself to walk forward.

The stark light made his tanned body look an unnaturally blanched white. A white cloth had been placed over his bared chest and a small section of it was stained with blood. Reluctantly, Daisy lifted the cloth and winced at the sight of a small incision in the chest. But it was the bruise on his chest that almost buckled her knees. It was enormous and in the shape of a hand.

A hand.

That meant that everything she had heard was right. William had been murdered. The thought caused her knees to finally give way and she slumped to the metal floor, howling and screaming her misery.

'How dare you!'

Captain Hawkins punched his fist angrily onto the desk.

Neither Erimem nor Sergeant Dorward were in the slightest bit impressed by the captain's show of outrage.

'Sit down please, captain,' Dorward said. There was a definite edge of steel to Dorward's apparently polite request.

Hawkins did as he was told, but did so with considerable bad grace. 'I object most strongly to being questioned this way. I'm the captain of this ship and I'm the one who asked you to handle this investigation.' He sniffed. 'I must admit I am now beginning to doubt the wisdom of that decision.'

'Do you regret allowing good to be smuggled on your ship?' Erimem asked bluntly.

'That is an outrageous accusation!' Hawkins blustered.

Erimem eyed him coolly. 'It will be outrageous if it is true.' She was standing at Dorward's shoulder. 'Sergeant, is smuggling a criminal offence?'

'It is,' Dorward nodded. 'It's punishable by imprisonment, and even if there were no charges brought, I imagine anyone guilty of smuggling on this ship would be immediately dismissed by the shipping line.' He paused briefly. 'Anything you would like to tell us, Captain Hawkins?'

Hawkins swallowed hard but said nothing. He simply shook his head.'

'As you wish,' Dorward said. 'Back to the beginning then.'

Captain Hawkins' shoulders slumped.

'So, this is the swankiest suite on the ship?'

Helena gave Andy a disapproving look. 'You just wanted to say "swankiest suite" didn't you?'

Andy grinned in reply. 'I just wanted to say "swankiest". The "suite" was a Brucie Bonus.'

'He's obviously minted, isn't he?' Ibrahim was picking his way through the clothes in Etheridge's wardrobe, while Helena and Andy looked around other parts of the suite.

Helena nodded. 'Owns more businesses than Richard Branson, as wealthy as Bill Gates and as much of a posh twat as Jacob Rees-...'

'Ah-ah...' Andy interrupted. 'We do not mention his name.'

Helena smiled indulgently. 'It's worse than Betelgeuse.'

'I'd rather have Betelgeuse paying us a visit,' Andy sniffed.

Helena moved the conversation back on track. 'How much research did you do when you went and got our super secret service passes?'

'A fair bit,' Ibrahim's voice came from the wardrobe. 'We had to avoid reading the end of things, so we don't know how things end up here.'

Andy nodded. 'Don't want us messing things up by trying to stick to history. But we did come up with a bit of backstory for Lord Twattingdon and a few others on the ship.'

'Not all,' Ibrahim added, 'but some.'

Helena had moved across to another wardrobe. 'God, he's got more clothes than me. He's probably got more clothes here than I've ever owned.'

'He's also got a diary,' Andy said from the desk. She had found a stack of papers and notebooks.

Ibrahim moved across to join her. 'So? Most businessmen do.' He flipped open a notebook and closed it in disgust. 'This is private. Quite offensively so.'

'How do you mean?' asked Helena.

Andy took the notebook from Ibrahim and skimmed a few pages. 'It seems that Lord Wanker is a womaniser... and he keeps notes on his conquests.'

Helena was outraged. 'What?'

Andy passed the book across. 'See for yourself.'

Helena flipped through a few pages, scanning just a few lines on each page. 'That's vile.'

'He's a pervert,' Andy snarled.

'And for one so young, you are a prude.' They spun to find Etheridge standing in his doorway. 'And I would call myself a connoisseur rather than a pervert.'

'Does a connoisseur grade women like cattle?' Helena demanded.

Etheridge walked into his suite. 'Only one who can afford to do so. Now get out.'

'We're not finished,' Andy said

'You're finished.' Etheridge pulled a pistol from his pocket and aimed it at his unwelcome visitors. 'And when I get home I'll make sure your careers are finished.'

Ibrahim began easing his friends towards the door. 'I think he's willing to use that.'

'I'm damned sure he is,' answered Helena quietly.

Etheridge waved the pistol towards the door. 'Before I have

to prove you correct, get out.'

At the door Helena paused. 'You know how it looks, threatening people carrying out an official investigation?'

Etheridge snorted. 'I don't care how it looks. Just get out.'

'All right,' Andy nodded, 'we're going – but the next time we meet you might well be in handcuffs.'

'And you might be the Queen of England but you're not,' Etheridge sneered. 'Anderson!' he called and his servant appeared in the doorway. 'If these interlopers come back again, shoot them.'

'Shoot them, sir?'

'You heard.'

Helena stared coldly at Etheridge. 'Try it and we'll throw you in jail.'

Etheridge answered quickly. 'Refuse and I'll throw you out of work.'

Ibrahim eased Helena and Andy out of the door. 'Don't worry, Mr Anderson, we won't cost you your job.'

'But we will talk to you later,' Helena added.

She let that hang in the air as a threat as Ibrahim pulled the door closed.

The interviews with the rest of the First Class passengers and crew ran for the remainder of the morning and deep into the afternoon. Unfortunately, despite hours of questioning, nobody was able or willing to provide any kind of answer. Everyone was on holiday or heading home from a business trip or vacation. Everyone had been fond of Mr Carlisle but they had no idea of why anyone would want to harm him, and none of them had any idea at all about any kind of smuggling.

The crew's affection for Carlisle was also evident. He had been a gent and the First Officer but he had treated them well. Both Erimem and Dorward had been convinced, however that some of the crew were very aware of a smuggling operation – but they were equally sure that none of them knew of an ape being transported aboard the ship. The crew's reactions had varied from startled by the thought to being openly amused, but none of them appeared to believe it true.

Helena, Ibrahim and Andy had joined the group in the small lounge and reported their progress or more precisely their lack of success.

'No smoking gun,' Andy confessed sadly. 'Or giant banana or whatever.'

Helena sank into a chair. 'But if there's a giant beastie on board it has to be somewhere.'

'I do not think the crew know of it,' Erimem answered. 'If they do their eyes lie very well. But we did have a thought.'

'A trap?' suggested Andy.

'Exactly,' Erimem humphed in disappointment. 'How did you know?'

Andy smiled affectionately at her friend. 'We know you and how that brain of yours works. So what's the plan?'

Sergeant Dorward glanced at Erimem and at her silent invitation took up the explanation. 'The crew are being kept in First Class for another twenty minutes. There are three we think are most likely to be involved. They reacted most when smuggling was mentioned.'

Erimem took over. 'We will follow them and when one or more of them goes to see if their... what word would you use?'

'Contraband?' suggested Andy.

Erimem nodded. 'That is it. Contraband. When they go to find their contraband, we follow and arrest them.'

'Do we also arrest the murderous gorilla?' asked Andy.

Erimem rubbed her chin thoughtfully. 'We will have to come up with a plan for that.'

The body of First Officer William Carlisle lay still, silent and alone in in the empty cargo hold. The door creaked slowly open and a large, powerful figure entered, looking around, sniffing the air, searching for any sign that there was any other life in the hold.

After a moment, the figure accepted that there was no-one but Carlisle in the room. It hurried across the metal floor until it stood beside the table holding the dead man.

The cloth over Carlisle's chest was lifted with a sort of vague curiosity then dropped haphazardly across his chest again.

A large powerful hand lifted one of Carlisle's hands and raised it so that it could be sniffed. It was still for a moment before sliding the thumb of the First Officer's hand into its mouth. Large, strong teeth sheared through flesh, muscle and bone, biting the thumb cleanly off.

Releasing Carlisle's hand, the figure turned and left the cargo hold.

What had started as an unexpected and slightly unwelcome promotion in duties for Junior Lieutenant Arthur Mills had become a chore. He had been due to come off duty almost two hours earlier but word had come from the captain that Mills was to stay on duty as officer of the watch until further notice.

What did that mean?

Until somebody else could be bothered to turn up?

Until the old man himself managed to peel his brandy-soaked carcass away from the diners in First Class?

Maybe until Mr Carlisle came back on duty. There had been rumours aboard ship in the last few hours that something had happened to Mr Carlisle. Talk about Carlisle and young Daisy as well. Mills hadn't expected that to be true. If he was honest he was rather disappointed in Mr Carlisle about that. A First Officer should have his eyes aimed higher than a mere maid. It would damage Carlisle's career, that was for sure.

It also explained why Daisy had constantly rebuffed Mills' own approaches.

He looked around his crew on the bridge. They were a different lot from earlier in the day but they had the same surly looks on their faces. This had all the signs of being a very long night.

The door opened and a familiar neatly uniformed figure strode onto the bridge. Relief flooded through Mills along with resentment and he straightened his back to greet his superior 'Sir,' he said formally.'

'Dismissed,' was the only reply.

Dismissed? That was his thanks for taking on another man's duty?

Mills answered sharply with a crisp 'Sir!' before striding out of the bridge. He made his way below decks and headed for the mess. As he had feared the chef had retired for the night, though a selection of cold food had been left out for crew coming off duty. It was late and the lights were low, but Mills filled his plate high with chicken and ham, potatoes, carrots and tomatoes. It was an odd mixture which would have appalled Chef, but Mills didn't care. He was hungry and he had earned the right to eat whatever he wanted, even if it was these leftovers from the First Class table.

Sitting himself at a table, Mills thought that he was the only person in the dull room, but as a fork laden with ham approached his mouth he heard a noise from the shadows. Peering into the dark he saw a solitary figure slumped in a chair. It was undoubtedly one of the female members of the crew and, more annoyingly, she was crying. Damn it, that was all he needed. Why did they let women on board a ship if they couldn't control their emotions?

Oh, God, she had seen him.

'I'm sorry.' Her voice was thick and she choked even on those short words. He recognised the voice as belonging to Daisy Brown.

'It's fine,' Mills answered, returning his attention to the meal which was quickly losing its appeal.

'It's just... you know...'

Oh, God, she wasn't going to try to talk to him about whatever was bothering her, was she?

Apparently she was.

'It's just a bit of a shock,' she said in a dull, thick voice. 'I can't believe it. Not William... Mr Carlisle.'

Oh, so that was it. The First Officer had seen sense and dropped her. He might take a look at her again later himself if he didn't find someone better. He would have to wait to let the taint of her being Carlisle's girl fade. He didn't want to be known for accepting cast offs.

'It happens,' Mills said, hoping that would be an end of the conversation.

He was out of luck.

'It happens?' Daisy asked incredulously. 'Mr Carlisle is murdered on board this ship and all you can say is that it happens?'

Mills stared at Daisy as if she were quite mad. 'What are you talking about? Mr Carlisle's not dead.'

'He is,' Daisy insisted vehemently. 'I saw his body last night.'

'And I saw him on the bridge about ten minutes ago,' Mills answered impatiently. 'He relieved me as officer of the watch.'

Daisy looked utterly shocked. 'But I saw him.'

'So did I!'

'On the bridge?' Daisy asked urgently.

Mills sighed with irritation. 'That's what I said. Why don't...'

There was no point in him continuing. Daisy was running for the door. Mills snorted, convinced that he was lucky to have avoided falling in with the girl. She was obviously highly strung or needy. Or just a lunatic. Whatever it was, he didn't care. He just wanted his dinner.

Daisy ran through the ship's corridors.

What Lieutenant Mills had said made no sense. She had seen Will's body. He had been dead. That woman doctor had said so. Doctor Griffiths had agreed with her. How could they have been wrong? Could it have been a trick? Punishing her for loving someone above her station? No, nobody would be as cruel as that, and Will Carlisle would never be party to anything that would hurt her. They had discussed marriage – she had accepted his proposal – and she was going to meet his family. He simply wasn't capable of that kind of cruelty.

She ran through the nearly deserted corridors, taking three flights of steps on her way to the bridge. She had reached the deck on which the bridge was situated when she saw a familiar, impossible, figure standing in front of her at the far end of the corridor.

'Will?' The tall man didn't turn until she repeated his name. 'Will?'

William Carlisle looked up and showed no reaction as Daisy threw herself into his arms. She didn't care if anyone saw them. She gripped him tightly, pulling him into an embrace.

Carlisle said nothing.

'Will? What happened? They said you were dead. I saw you. You looked like you were gone. What happened?'

Carlisle still didn't reply. There was a look of concentration on his face as he scrutinised her face. He seemed unsure, so unlike the confident man she loved. Whatever had happened to him, there was still something very wrong.

'Should you be up?' Daisy asked. 'You don't look well.

'I am... fine.' He seemed have had to search for the word. His voice was distant. 'Yes, that is it,' he said carefully. 'I am fine.' His frown deepened as he peered at her face more intently. 'Daisy. I am fine, *Daisy.*'

She had always loved the way Will Carlisle said her name. He made it sound playful and exciting. It always made her smile when she heard him say her name.

This time it didn't make her smile.

A chill as cold as ice ran down her spine and Daisy Brown began to tremble.

Will Carlisle looked at her with unfocused, glassy eyes.

Daisy wanted to scream but the sound wouldn't come.

CHAPTER SEVEN

The three members of the ship's crew who had been identified as potentially aware of a smuggling operation were, as planned, followed by members of the investigation team after they were given permission to leave First Class. To the annoyance to both Helena and Erimem, Sergeant Dorward had insisted upon taking part in the operation. Unwilling to be left alone, Nadia Bakshi also demanded to be involved. In the end, Helena and Nadia followed a small ginger-haired man by the name of Onions while Andy and Ibrahim tailed Brodie and a tall, almost skeletal steward by the name of Walters was followed by Erimem and Dorward.

While he undoubtedly struggled to keep up the pace, Dorward offered no complaint about the pain from his injury and showed remarkable skill at staying out of view of their prey.

Walters was a wine steward and from the distance of a corridor Erimem and Dorward heard the man say to a colleague that he was heading down to the wine cellar. That was obviously some kind of in-joke because it produced a bark of laughter from the other crewman.

As they moved deeper into the guts of the ship, the polish and shine that was so much part of life above decks disappeared, replaced by oil and grime.

Dorward's face wore a heavy sheen of sweat by the time Walters finally stopped after winding his way through the twisting innards of the ship. After looking around to ensure, wrongly as it transpired, that he was alone, Walters quickly opened a padlock and pushed the door open. He quickly slipped inside.

Erimem and Dorward followed quietly and paused at the door.

'Are you ready?' she asked.

'I should be asking you,' Dorward muttered.

Erimem gave a small smile. 'Then I assume we are both ready.' She pushed the door open and stepped through.

Walters was standing in a large, wide hold, surrounded by crates. He looked up, startled by their appearance. 'You shouldn't be here,' he flustered.

'From the expression on your face,' Erimem replied, 'I would say that you should not be here either.'

The steward regained some of his composure. 'This area is off limits to passengers. You should go back above decks. I'll show you the way...'

'Very kind of you,' Dorward replied, 'and we'll take you up on that...'

Erimem completed the answer, '...after we have seen what is stored in here.'

'Nothing important,' Walters answered.

'Do you believe him?' Erimem asked lightly.

'Not even wee bit,' Dorward answered, staring hard at Walters. 'So, would you like to try again?'

The steward buckled. 'Look, I'm only a steward. I do what I'm told.'

'Good,' Erimem said. 'You can do as you're told and open these crates.'

'I'll get the sack if I do.'

'You'll get arrested if you don't,' Dorward assured him.

'All right.' Walters reached for a crowbar which rested on top of a wooden crate. It was blatantly clear from his expression that he was wondering if he could possibly use it to make a run.

'If you try anything foolish with that,' Erimem said quietly, 'I will take that from you and use it to break your arms.'

Walters believed her. He drew his hand away from the crate.

Dorward pointed to a corner of the hold. 'Stand there, you.' Lifting the crowbar he prised the top off of the nearest crate.

Erimem reached past him and lifted stone statues from the straw inside the crate. 'This is ancient,' she said. 'Egyptian.' She turned her cold gaze to Walters. 'These have been looted from tombs.'

'I dunno what's in there,' Walters whined.

'But you know who it belongs to,' said Erimem.

The steward shook his head. 'That side's nothing to do with me.'

'Is there any paperwork for these crates?' Dorward asked.

Walters shook her head again. 'None.'

'Wait,' Erimem said. A label was stuck to the lid Dorward had pushed aside. 'There is a paper stuck to the crate.' She read it quickly. 'It has writing on it.'

Dorward peered at the paper. 'An address?'

Erimem frowned and shook her head in disappointment. 'Not really. It has "London" on it. Nothing else.'

Dorward humphed. 'That's a big address.'

Erimem had already moved to the next crate. 'This says "London" as well.' She moved to the next. 'This is different,' she said with interest.'

The third crate was marked with three letters.

UWH.

'Code?' Erimem asked.

Dorward's lips pursed. 'I'm not sure. Can you remember the addresses of the people up in First Class?'

Erimem wasn't sure that she could remember them all. And what did they have to do with... Dorward's meaning fell into place. 'Upper Westleigh Manor?' she asked. 'UWM... Upper Westleigh Manor?'

Dorward nodded. 'Upper Westleigh Manor. That would mean that these smuggled goods belong to...'

Erimem smiled grimly. 'Lord Etheridge.'

'And he has a house in London,' Dorward agreed. 'This isn't absolute proof but it's a beginning. We have to talk to Etheridge again.'

'Yes,' Erimem agreed, 'and this time he will not be so insulting.' She turned to Walters. 'Are there any other places on board the ship like this? Places where you smuggle other things?'

'Like wild animals maybe?' Dorward added.

Walters looked confused.

Returning to the upper decks, Erimem and Dorward found that the other two teams of Helena and Nadia, and Ibrahim and Andy had have beaten them back.

'We have made a discovery,' Erimem said excitedly. She stopped as she saw the grim faces of her friends. 'What is wrong?'

They stepped aside and Erimem saw lying on the floor, with her neck twisted at a grotesque angle, her eyes wide and staring, was the dead body of the maid, Daisy Brown.

'Her neck's broken,' Helena said. 'The head has almost been twisted off.'

'Did anyone witness the killing?' Erimem asked.

Andy shook her head. 'Not as far as we can tell. We haven't questioned everybody yet.'

'We have sent for the captain, though,' Helena added.

Erimem drew a deep breath, drawing her thoughts into order. 'Good, because we very much need to talk with him. About this and about the smuggling on his ship.'

'What did you find?' Ibrahim asked.

It was Dorward who answered. Three small compartments in the hold, all of them used for smuggling.'

'But there is no wild animal being smuggled on the ship that the steward knows about,' Erimem finished.

'So who the hell's doing the King Kong impersonation?' asked Andy.

Captain Hawkins wore a façade of outrage as he strode into the lounge, which had again become the base of the investigation.

'What in the devil do you mean by dragging me here?' he demanded.

'Please sit down, captain,' Dorward said coolly. He was again seated at a table with Nadia at his side ready to take notes.

'I will not sit down!' Hawkins barked. 'I'm putting an end to this nonsense. I should never have let you take this investigation. I'll take control of it till we reach Southampton.'

Nobody was put off by Hawkins' bluster. They had known it was coming. 'No, you will not,' Erimem said. She was leaning against an ornately decorated pillar. 'You will answer our questions about the historical artefacts being smuggled in the hold of your ship.'

Hawkins blanched. 'I don't know what you're talking about.'

'You are lying,' Erimem answered sharply. 'The steward informed us that the order for these crates to be brought on board was handed to him by you.'

'A captain should know everything that happens on his ship,' Dorward said. 'Even the illegal activities.'

Erimem turned to Andy. 'Talking of illegal action, Etheridge should be brought here.'

A smile crossed Andy's face. 'He'll be in his pit. He won't enjoy being wakened.'

'He might make good on his threat to shoot us,' Ibrahim warned.

Dorward looked hard at Captain Hawkins. 'I assume you have an arms locker in case of emergencies?'

'Well, yes,' Hawkins answered uncomfortably, 'but you can't bring a member of the House of Lords here under armed guard.'

'Okay,' Andy said. 'We'll bring him in handcuffs instead.'

'No!' Hawkins looked horrified by the prospect. He tried to present a calm face. 'Look, I'm sure we can deal with all of this calmly, so that everybody comes out of it well.'

'Does that include Mr Carlisle and the maid, Daisy?' Helena asked quietly.

The question quietened Hawkins.

Erimem tapped Andy's arm. 'I will come with you. We will not need weapons, but we will take two of the stewards.'

That all seemed agreeable to Dorward. 'All right, but try to do it with the minimum of fuss.'

Andy moved towards the door. 'Don't worry. We can do subtle.'

Erimem seemed dubious at the claim. 'Can we? When did we learn to do that?'

'Ignore her.' Andy nudged Erimem towards the door. 'Come along, dearie.'

They had only just left when Ibrahim entered, with a weary junior officer in tow. Captain Hawkins frowned at the sight of his subordinate. 'What are you doing here, Mills? You're supposed to be on the bridge.'

Lieutenant Mills appeared confused by his captain's question. 'I was relieved, sir,' he answered.

'And wait till you hear who relieved him,' Ibrahim said.

'Well?' Hawkins demanded.

Dorward indicated a chair. 'Sit down, Lieutenant, and tell us who relieved you.'

Mills sat on a chair and looked irritably at the faces around him. 'It was Mr Carlisle.'

'Impossible,' Hawkins snapped.

Ibrahim shook his head. 'I went up to the bridge and checked with the crew up there. First Officer William Carlisle gave the order relieving Mills of his station.'

Hawkins spun to glare at Helena. 'You said he was dead. How could you be wrong about something as simple as that?'

'She wasn't,' Dorward said quickly, earning a nod of thanks from Helena. 'I inspected Mr Carlisle and so did your own ship's doctor. His neck was broken, his chest was crushed. Believe me, he was dead last night.'

Mills shook his head stubbornly. 'Well he was alive again about an hour and a bit since.'

Helena was heading for the door. 'There's only one way to find out who's right,' she said. 'We go and inspect the body.'

Dorward nodded and painfully pushed himself upright. 'We'll all do that.'

'I'm sorry, ladies,' Warren Anderson said to the two young women standing at the door of his employer's suite, 'His Lordship has retired to bed and I am under instructions not to disturb him tonight.'

'Nevertheless, he's required to answer more questions,' Andy replied cheerfully, 'so would you wake him please, or we certainly will?'

Anderson put on a final show of defiance. 'I'm afraid I simply can't let you in. I have my instruction.'

Andy sighed. 'Erimem, be a pal and threaten him, would you?'

'With pleasure.'

Erimem took a step closer... and Anderson took a step to the side.

'Good lad,' Andy smiled, following Erimem inside.

As Andy had told Erimem on the way to fetch Etheridge, his suite was a good deal more luxurious than anything else aboard ship. The place was spotless and the furniture and fitting looked as if they belonged on a much swankier ship.

Anderson pointed to a door on the left. 'He's in that one, but he has been in there for a time. I haven't seen him in over an hour. He hates having his sleep disturbed.' He wrung his hands. 'He will be so angry at being wakened. I'll lose my job.'

Erimem pushed the door open and operated the light switch. 'I think he would be very pleased if we could wake him,' she said.

Something in her friend's tome made Andy hurry to her side.

Lord Etheridge lay sprawled on a rug by the bed. His neck had been twisted so violently that the skin had torn under the strain.

'Oh...' Anderson looked past the woman at his dead employer. 'Oh, my...'

'How did the killer get in?' Erimem asked Anderson. 'How did they killer get past you to murder this man?'

'Were you in the suite all the time since Etheridge went to bed?' Andy asked.

'Yes,' Anderson nodded, then shook his head as a memory came to him. 'Well, except for ten minutes when I took His Lordship's instructions for breakfast to the kitchen. He had complained that the eggs weren't quite right.'

'And you were gone for ten minutes?' Erimem asked. 'No more?'

'Maybe fifteen?' Anderson suggested.

'And someone knew that they should come into this suite and kill your employer in exactly those fifteen minutes?' Erimem asked. She made no effort to hide her lack of trust in Anderson's tale.

'Did you see anybody when you were out of the suite?' Andy asked.

Anderson nodded vigorously. There was something about the one they called Erimem that made him very nervous. He had no doubts that she would torture him if she thought it necessary. She had been more than eager to threaten him at her friend's request. 'I met with a couple of the cooks. They weren't happy and had something to say about His Lordship's requests. I saw a few members of the crew as I went and came back, and rather a lot of the passengers were still milling about. I saw a good number of people. I should be happy to list them, if you wish.'

Erimem nodded, apparently accepting Anderson's explanation. 'Have you been in every room in the suite yet?'

'No, why?' Anderson blanched visibly. 'You think the killer might still be here?'

'I think we should find out,' Erimem said firmly.

The body of First Officer William Carlisle lay still and unmoving in the cool hold that had been assigned for use as an examination room and morgue. Lying on a second table a few feet to the side, reunited in death with her love was Daisy Brown.

Lieutenant Arthur Mills stared at the corpses in confusion. 'I don't understand. I saw him not long ago. And I saw her – Daisy – alive a few minutes later.'

'We know you did,' Ibrahim said. 'Nobody doubts you. The crew back you up.'

'How?' Mills repeated in a faltering voice.

Dorward eased forward uncomfortably on his sticks. 'That's a good question.'

'Here's another good question,' Helena said, lifting Carlisle's hand so that everyone could see the mutilation to the dead man's hand. 'Who the hell cut his thumb off?'

'And why?' added Dorward.

'I'll tell you how,' Helena said. She pointed at the curved, ridged edge of the wound. 'That's a bite wound. You can see the marks of the teeth.'

'Let me see.' Dorward hobbled closer to observe the wound. 'You're right. It's definitely a bite. It's not like anything I've seen before, though. I've seen dogs biting me, I've seen men bite other men. I've even seen horse and pig bites. This is different.'

Helena agreed. 'Crocodile, lizard, bird of prey... I've seen some, too and I agree. This is totally new to me.' She pointed at the bone. 'Look at how cleanly it's been bitten through. The teeth must have been incredibly sharp... and strong, too, to withstand that kind of bite pressure.'

Dorward rubbed at the stubble on his chin nervously. 'Can you think of any animal that has a sort of bite fingerprint like this?'

'No,' Helena answered.

'Arse,' Dorward breathed. 'I cannae think of anything either. And it looks big.'

Helena nodded. 'The teeth are big, rounded for tearing meat and bone.'

Captain Hawkins shook his head in confusion. 'This makes no sense.'

Dorward turned angrily on the captain. 'What animal are you smuggling for Etheridge?'

'Nothing,' Hawkins flustered. 'I'm not...'

Helena interrupted his bluster. 'Either you answer us or Etheridge does, but either way somebody will answer.'

'It will not be Etheridge.' Erimem's voice came from the door. 'He is dead.' She moved into the room with Andy behind her. Warren Anderson nervously brought up the rear.

Dorward was first to react. 'What happened?'

'He was murdered,' Andy answered. 'Pretty nastily.'

Hawkins looked grey. 'His Lordship is dead? On my ship?'

Dorward turned his attention to the ship's captain. 'And if you're smuggling for him, that puts you right at the top of our list of suspects.'

'But I didn't kill him,' Hawkins protested. 'Why would I? He hasn't paid me yet.'

'How do we know that's true?' Erimem demanded.

'Ask *him*,' Hawkins said, pointing at Warren Anderson. 'He knows all about Lord Etheridge's transactions. He even handles some of them.'

'Only the minor ones,' Anderson protested. 'I'm a very minor member of His Lordship's staff.'

'But you are the only one here with him,' Erimem said. 'That means you were useful to him.'

'Is there a list of his transactions?' Erimem asked.

Anderson nodded uncertainly.

That was enough for Dorward. 'I want every bit of Etheridge's paperwork on the table upstairs in five minutes.'

CHAPTER EIGHT

'I had no idea,' Captain Hawkins said quickly.

Every pair of eyes in the room was on the sailor and none looked as if they believed him.

'Really?' Andy's eyebrow lifted sarcastically. 'You had no idea that His Scumbag Lordship had booked and paid for the journeys of almost everybody in First Class?'

'That's right,' Hawkins nodded furiously.

Erimem seemed no more convinced by the denials. 'Is that a normal thing for Lord Etheridge or anyone else to do?'

'Damned generous of him,' Helena said softly. 'We should have told him we were sailing First Class. Maybe he'd have footed the bill for us as well.'

'Well?' Dorward demanded of Warren Anderson. 'Was your employer a generous man given to spending his money on people this way?'

Anderson shook his head quickly. 'Not at all, sir. In fact I should say he was rather careful with his money... when it came to other people.'

'So he was happy to splash out and spend big on himself?' asked Andy.

Anderson agreed quickly. 'Oh, yes, miss. He always said as it was his money and he deserved the benefits of it.'

'So why did he spend money on these people?' Erimem wondered, 'Unless...'

'Unless there was something in it for him,' Helena and Andy chorused.

Erimem nodded. 'Exactly. That would mean there was some

kind of connection between Etheridge and these people.'

'I think we should find out what those links are,' Dorward said, squaring his shoulders. 'And find out why the Hell they didn't tell us about those links when we interviewed them earlier.'

'Yes, I knew Etheridge before this voyage,' said Countess Olga Bischkova. She sat ramrod straight, looking across the table at Dorward. She had glanced at the others in the room before sitting but now paid them no heed. 'I did not deny this.'

'You didn't mention in our first interview that you didn't buy your own tickets either,' Dorward said.

The Countess gave no reaction but remained impassive for just a moment too long. 'That is no-one's business but mine,' she said.

'Yours and Lord Etheridge's,' Dorward countered, 'given that it was him who paid for the tickets for you and your daughter.'

Countess Bischkova winced.

'You did not know he was the one who supplied the tickets,' said Erimem. It was a statement rather than a question.

'No,' the Countess conceded, 'I did not. They were delivered as being from...' she sought exactly the right word, '...from an admirer or a friend.'

'Do all your friends and admirers have expensive taste?' asked Dorward.

Olga Bischkova looked momentarily uncomfortable. She glanced around all of those facing her. 'Is it usual for so many people to interrogate one innocent woman?'

'Is it usual for you to avoid answering questions?' Erimem replied sharply.

Olga Bischkova straightened her back definatly. 'In my country I was a countess. I will not be spoken to in this manner.'

Andy snorted and nodded towards Erimem. 'Countess? In her country Erimem was a queen. Queen trumps countess.'

Dorward looked bemused at the revelation about Erimem's position but Erimem herself was focused on Countess Bischkova. 'So, will you answer my question?'

The Countess took a moment to square her shoulders. 'The revolution fragmented our strata of Russian society. We are scattered across the world. We help each other as best we can. It has been no secret that I have wanted to relocate to England for some time.'

'Why?' asked Dorward.

'Because you still have a monarchy,' Countess Olga Bischkova answered. 'You still have respect for the old structures of society.'

Andy's eyebrow lifted. 'You mean that those born into aristocracy still have privilege?'

'That would make us think that you would like Etheridge,' Erimem said thoughtfully, 'or at least share some kind of kinship with one of your own class.' She glanced apologetically at Andy. 'I apologise for breaking this into class. I know it is something you loathe.'

Andy waved a hand dismissively. 'Carry on, love. Knock yourself out.'

Erimem continued with her thoughts. 'You reacted coldly when you were placed at the Captain's Table with Etheridge. We all saw that.' She leaned forward. 'But you were furious when he took your daughter to dance. So angry that you struck him... you struck the only other person of your class on the ship. Why did you do that?'

'I do not have to answer that.'

'Yes, you do, Countess,' Dorward said coldly. 'This is a murder investigation. 'You do not get to choose which questions you do or do not answer.'

Andy had flipped through a heavy notebook and now set it on the table. 'This is Etheridge's travel ledger,' she said. 'Mr Anderson and his predecessor use it to keep track of plans for Etheridge's travels.' She flipped open a page from several years earlier. 'He was in Singapore in 1919.'

'As were you,' Erimem added. 'Did you meet him there?'

A cold anger had crept into Olga Bischkova's eyes. 'I met many people in Singapore. A great many of my people fled the revolution. I met a good number in Singapore.'

'That was definitely an answer to a question,' Erimem said, 'but it was not an answer to the question I asked. I will repeat it.

Did you meet Etheridge in Singapore in 1919?'

'Yes,' Countess Bischkova said in a brittle voice. 'Yes, I met him.'

'And he offended you so badly that you were afraid for your daughter to even dance with him?' Erimem pressed.

Countess Bischkova took a moment before answering. 'The man is a pig. I will never let him near my daughter.'

'One question,' Andy said softly. 'How old is your daughter?'

'She is not part of this conversation.'

'I think she might be,' Andy said. 'You told us you were pregnant when you left Russia.'

'Yes.'

'Then you must be in the record books for the longest pregnancy in history.' She held up Bischkova's passport. If the dates you gave for leaving Russia and your husband dying are accurate, you must have been pregnant for about seventeen months.'

'Are you questioning my word?'

Andy closed the book. 'I'm questioning your maths.'

'And,' Erimem interjected rather more gently, 'perhaps she is questioning the behaviour of Etheridge when he met you in Singapore.'

Olga Bischkova broke. 'Do I have your word that none of this will leave this room and it will never be spoken of again?'

Dorward nodded solemnly. 'If you're not involved in any of the criminal events then everyone here will keep the matter private.' He spoke quietly to the young woman at his side. 'Nadia... Miss Bakshi, would you leave this part out of your notes, please?'

Nadia put her pen down immediately. 'Of course.'

Dorward invited Ola Bischkova to begin. 'Countess?'

Reluctantly, the Russian gave way. 'Very well. When I arrived in Singapore I had very little. I had several loyal soldiers and the crew of my yacht but they were reliant on me for their futures. I had few possessions and little in the way of gold or money, yet I was the one to whom everyone turned. We were welcome in very few places back then. After Nicholas, the Tsar, abdicated, even Britain refused to take him in. We were outcasts and vulnerable. I needed to find a way for us to survive in Singapore at least for a time. I sold my yacht for less than half of its worth but I had no choice. I invested my money by buying three nightclubs. They seemed elegant and prosperous but I was misled about the nature of the clubs. People did not come for music or to drink. *People* did not come at all. *Men* came, and paid for what they wanted.'

'You bought a chain of brothels,' Helena said.

'No. I bought clubs,' Olga Bischkova protested.

Helena persisted, 'In which men paid women to have sex.'

'There is no need to be so crude,' Bischkova snapped.

Helena shrugged. 'It's a pretty crude business.'

'As I informed you, I was misled,' the Countess said, 'but I made the best of them. I made my clubs of a higher class, where the music and ambience would appeal.'

'So you went for an up-market clientele?' Andy asked.

Helena still seemed unconvinced that Countess Olga Bischkova was an unwilling dupe. 'Who would pay more for their pleasure? Unless you ended the bedroom shenanigans.'

Bischkova flushed a deep red. 'Almost all of the girls who worked in the clubs were Russian. They came to us because they knew my men would protect them. They would be safe.'

Helena remained unimpressed. 'Interesting definition of safe.'

Bischkova stared at Helena with a cold fury. 'You have no right to judge us. We did what was necessary.'

Helena met the woman's gaze evenly. 'I'm sure they did.'

'The girls made good money,' the Countess protested. 'They were able to save.'

'And *you* made good money, too?' Andy asked.

'Yes. I...' Bischkova baulked at the perceived suggestion that she had been available to the men. 'No, I did not do that. I was not one of those girls.'

Andy shrugged. 'Didn't say you were.'

Erimem had no interest in Bischkova's hurt feelings. 'So what happened with Etheridge?'

'He came to my club. What he wanted, he was told he could not have. He did not think that the rules of life applied to him. He did not think people should say no to him. He did not hear it very often.'

Erimem nodded her understanding. 'And you said no to him?'

'I tried. He did not listen. Do I need to explain further?'

'No,' Erimem answered. 'You do not.'

'The result was your daughter?' Dorward asked. 'Does she know the truth?'

'No. She believes her father was a Russian hero. My husband. I trust she will continue to believe this.'

'We won't tell her,' Dorward promised.

'Did Etheridge know?' Helena asked.

Bischkova shook her head. 'No. Nobody knew. Nobody knew what he... what happened. If my men had known they would have killed him. He was involved with smuggling, and with the local gangs. They are very cruel, violent people. If Etheridge was killed we would have been at war with them. When I found I was pregnant...' She shrugged. 'I have my daughter. She is mine and her father was my husband. I never saw Etheridge again.'

'Wait,' said Andy, 'if Etheridge didn't know about your daughter why did he buy you these tickets?'

'I do not know.'

'Did you see him in Alexandria?' Helena asked.

'No. I did not know he was here.'

'What were you doing in Alexandria?' asked Dorward.

'Singapore became difficult for Russians in the 1920s.' Olga Bischkova winced at the memories. 'We were doing too well. The gangs began to see us as a threat. They made life difficult. I had a daughter and she was all that mattered, so I gave in. I sold my clubs to the gangs. I bought hotels and nightclubs in Alexandria. Nightclubs without the other kinds of entertainment.'

That all made sense to Andy. 'You went legit,' she said.

Bischkova ignored the interruption. 'I have been in Alexandria for four years, but I see change coming. The same change that came in Russia. The people there are beginning to rebel. They are growing tired of Europe's interference. This time I think it best to leave before I have to run. My friends knew I had sold my clubs and hotels. They knew I was leaving. That is why I was not surprised to receive the tickets.'

A frown creased Dorward's brow and his finger tapped the table absent-mindedly. 'Etheridge must have found out about you when he was on holiday in Alexandria.'

'And then found out about your daughter,' added Erimem.

'Do you think he plans to take her from me?' Bischkova's voice rose in panic. 'I will never allow that to happen. I will kill him before I allow that to happen.'

'I'm afraid you're too late,' Dorward told her. 'Etheridge was found dead in his suite earlier tonight.'

Olga Bischkova froze in shock. 'What? How is he dead?'

'He was murdered,' Dorward answered quietly.

'Good...' the word came from the Cuntess without a thought, 'but also not so good. I am a suspect for his murder now?'

Dorward nodded. 'After what you said, I would say yes.'

Andy tried to lighten the mood. 'On the other hand, if you're innocent in this you'll be pleased to know it was a horrible, painful death.'

'No, I am not pleased,' Bischkova snapped. 'I hated him. He was a disgusting pig but I would rather he had suffered in life than an easy death.'

There was no denying the hate in Olga Bischkova's voice or her despair that any hope she had of making her attacker face the law had gone.

Dorward chose to bring the interview to a halt. 'That should be enough for now, except for one thing. While you had the hotels and clubs, did you happen to see anyone in any of those establishments who is now no board the *Agamemnon*?'

'Yes,' Bischcova answered, 'more than one.'

'Who?' Dorward asked.

'The loud and annoying colonel stayed a few times in one of my hotels I saw him in one of the nightclubs also.'

'Colonel Mackenzie?' Erimem queried.

The Countess nodded. 'That is him. I think he misunderstood the type of club it was.'

Dorward jotted a note in his small black notebook. 'Can you remember the dates he stayed at your hotel?'

'Only approximately, but I can tell you who to contact at the hotel to find out He is Russian. He will tell you if you use my name.'

'Thank you,' Dorward answered. 'Let's find out also who paid for his stay in the hotel.'

'There's no need,' said Warren Anderson who had been sitting quietly in the shadows at the edge of the light. 'I can tell you that.'

'Colonel Mackenzie, please stop lying to us.'

Mackenzie snapped back to his feet and towered over Dorward. 'I'm an officer and a gentleman. I'll not be spoken to like that. If you weren't a cripple I'd take you outside and give you a thrashing.'

Dorward didn't back down. 'If I wasn't on sticks I'd happily go outside with you and show you how we fight dirty on the streets.'

Erimem rose from her seat. 'If you wish to fight someone, Colonel Mackenzie, I am more than willing to take Sergeant Dorward's place.'

'Absurd. I don't fight women.'

Erimem stared through the officer. 'How very fortunate for you.'

'But you did accept a First Class ticket from Lord Etheridge for this voyage back to Britain,' Dorward stated forcefully.

Before the soldier cold protest, Erimem hit him with more facts. 'And you also accepted accommodation in one of Alexandria's better hotels, paid for by Lord Etheridge on three occasions in the past two months.'

Mackenzie knew that he couldn't argue his way out of the corner her was in and reached for bluff instead. 'Well, what of it? A gentleman needs civilised conversation out here.'

Erimem's eyes narrowed with anger at the insult. 'Really?'

'So what did you discuss in these civilised conversations?' asked Helena.

'That's between Lord Etheridge and myself.'

'That being the Lord Etheridge you pretended not to know?' Helena shot back.

Mackenzie squared his shoulders, giving the appearance of a pillar of polite society. 'One doesn't make a show of being acquainted with the aristocracy. It's not the done thing.'

'Is smuggling for the aristocracy the done thing?' Erimem pushed.

Dorward scanned his notebook for a second. 'There are crates in a locked hold below decks – a hold used for smuggling as the ship's captain and several of the crew have reluctantly admitted – which contains crates of artefacts from Abu Bin Abim, which is, I believe, where you were stationed.'

Mackenzie's jaw jutted out defiantly. 'I know the allegations made against me and I'll face my accusers in a courts martial, not here on some tuppeny-ha'penny boat.' His eyes narrowed suspiciously. 'Unless the regiment has sent you lot to deal with me before we get back to England. Is that the way of it? Avoid the embarrassment of a courts martial by having me arrested on trumped up charges of smuggling here so they can waive jurisdiction? That's a fine way to treat an officer I must say. I'll not have it. And I'll be defended by the finest barristers in London.'

'Paid for by Lord Etheridge?' asked Erimem.

Mackenzie pointed an angry finger at Erimem. 'You be careful with what you say.'

'You are the one being questioned,' Erimem answered. 'You should be careful with what you say.'

'Lord Etheridge won't be providing you with any expensive legal counsel in London,' Dorward said nonchalantly.

'Or cheap counsel for that matter,' Andy added.

Mackenzie recognised the news as a blow but refused to be cowed. 'So he's a man of no integrity. Can't say it surprises me. I'll chat with him before we dock and he'll see to my solicitors.'

A humourless smile flitted across Andy's face. 'You're going to need a Ouija Board or at the very least a spirit medium.'

'What on Earth are you talking about, girl?' snapped Mackenzie.

'What I'm saying, slap-head,' Andy fired back, 'is that he's croaked. Snuffed it. He's not pining for the fjords, he's kicked the bucket.'

'Lord Etheridge was found dead not long ago,' Dorward confirmed,

The shock on Mackenzie's face seemed real enough. 'How?'

'Painfully,' Andy answered.

The soldier slammed his fists onto the table. 'Damn it all. The man was a scoundrel but I had no reason to wish him dead.'

'Except that you're facing a courts martial for smuggling for him?' said Dorward.

'The man assured me I'd never face a court,' Mackenzie snapped. 'He has influence in Whitehall.'

Dorward pursed his lips and sat back in his chair. 'He was going to cover it up and make it go away.'

Mackenzie straightened his back. 'Reckoned I'd simply be retired out on a good pension rather than have the army face the bad publicity of a trial.'

'Well, I think you'd better get ready for that bad publicity,' Andy said. 'Perhaps for more than smuggling.'

'You don't think I killed the man, do you?' demanded Mackenzie. 'I needed him alive.'

'Time will tell,' Dorward said.

Mackenzie leaned across the table, speaking urgently. 'If you want to know who to ask, you should have a word with Mrs Rollins.'

Dorward's mouth quirked into a sort of shrug. 'You seemed to be having quite a few words with her...'

'Or at her...' interrupted Andy.

'...during dinner on our first night out.' finished Dorward.

'Well, she was a lonely sort,' Mackenzie said magnanimously. 'Rather plain looking so she won't attract much interest. I kept her entertained with some old army tales.'

Helena stifled a laugh. 'I'm not sure "entertained" is the word that springs to mind.'

'Woman's a gold-digger,' Mackenzie said dismissively. 'She was only interested in asking about Etheridge. Her own husband is barely cold in his grave and she was eyeing a wealthy replacement.'

Dorward offered a false smile. 'We'll certainly invite Mrs Rollins in for a chat.'

'My name isn't Mary Rollins, I'm afraid.'

Sergeant Dorward's pen stopped, its tip against his notebook.

'It isn't?'

'No.'

Andy lifted a document from the table. 'Could you explain that to your passport? It thinks you are.'

The woman who wasn't Mary Rollins smiled warmly. 'Perhaps I should explain.'

'Perhaps you should,' Dorward said tightly.

'Here you go,' she said, handing over a small stack of papers drawn from inside her handbag. 'My real name is Audrey Marshall. I'm a journalist working for the London Evening Courier.'

'Good paper,' Helena said, 'as I recall anyway.'

'Thank you,' Audrey Marshall smiled curtly. 'We've had our eyes on Etheridge for a while. His name keeps cropping up on the edges of various shenanigans. It's never been enough to print anything concrete or land him in trouble with the law but he was worth investigating, and since nobody apart from that ghastly bore of a colonel gives a grieving widow a second look, tragic Mary Rollins was born.'

Andy dropped the fake passport onto the table. 'Along with her forged documents?'

'Forged-ish,' Audrey Marshall half-admitted.

'We'll come back to that,' said Dorward.

The confident smile didn't waver on Audrey's face. She looked – and indeed was – a completely different person having cast off her disguise. 'I'm sure we will.'

'So, what have you found out about Etheridge?' Erimem asked.

Audrey's lips pursed uncertainly. 'I will get into terrible trouble if spill the beans to you before I tell my editor.'

Dorward set his pen down very carefully. 'Miss Marshall, you might already be in terrible trouble.'

That only broadened the woman's smile. 'Oh, good. I do love a bit of trouble, don't you?'

'Not when it involved three murders,' Dorward snapped.

The smile disappeared and Audrey Marshall leaned forward with interest. 'Three? Who else is dead?'

'We'll come to that presently,' Dorward answered. 'Now, would you tell us what you know please?'

'And we have already spoken to Colonel Mackenzie.' Erimem added.

'Oh, bad luck,' Audrey said with feeling. He's ghastly, isn't he? Positively last century.''

'Perhaps two centuries ago,' Andy offered.

'Meckenzie's not a nice fellow,' Audrey continued. 'He enjoyed his time in the army because it let him bully and abuse natives.'

Andy snorted. 'He doesn't like people of colour.'

'No, he doesn't,' Audrey said, becoming serious, 'but that doesn't mean he's not partial to taking his pleasures with them.'

'Local prostitutes?' asked Erimem.

Audrey shook her head. 'He's an officer and a gentleman. So he says. He would never be quite as crass as that. No, he had an understanding of sorts with a woman at his previous posting. He kept her in a house, slid her enough money to live comfortably and at night she took care of him.'

'How cosy,' Helena said sourly.

Audrey Marshall grimaced and resumed her story. 'Until she told him that she was pregnant. He dropped her like a hot coal, stopped the money and had her thrown out of the house. When she went to see him at his barracks he had the men throw her out. She had faced a certain amount of resentment from the locals because of her association with Mackenzie. He wasn't a popular figure, and so she had no-one to offer her any sympathy or kindness when she needed it. She hung herself outside the house she had lived in. The locals found some sympathy for her then. They turned on the garrison which led to a few of them being shot. Officially it was all down to local troublemakers but some people knew the truth and for a few bribes in the right place, Lord Etheridge found out. He blackmailed Mackenzie into smuggling the pieces he wanted.'

Dorward inspected the words he had jotted down. 'Colonel Mackenzie kept a good deal of that back from us.'

'I'm not surprised,' Audrey answered. 'I can back it all up, though, and I imagine he's not the only one who's been holding back.'

Erimem's eyebrow arched in curiosity. 'Meaning?'

'Meaning your ship's doctor has a history of smuggling for

Etheridge on several ships,' Audrey replied.

'We'll have a chat with him about that,' Dorward assured her.

Audrey reached for her cigarette case then put it away again. 'No, I'm giving up,' she muttered before speaking in a more normal tone. 'You should also have a chat with Penelope Banks the socialite with her ever-so close chum, Lucy Isaac.'

'Are you insinuating they are more than friends?' asked Andy.

Audrey waved her hand dismissively. 'Oh, I'm stating it out loud. Not that there's anything wrong with it.'

'Too right,' Andy agreed. 'Don't knock what you haven't tried.'

Audrey eyed Andy with interest. 'Who says I haven't tried it? But we're straying from the topic at hand. The lovely Miss Banks has a tragic background.'

'We know her father committed suicide,' Erimem said. She made no attempt to hide her irritation when people drifted off topic.

'Yes,' Audrey agreed, 'but do you know it was Etheridge who drove him to it? Rather a coincidence that she's on this boat too, don't you think?'

'Not really,' replied Dorward, 'given that Etheridge paid for tickets for both of the ladies.'

'Oh, now that is interesting.' Audrey suddenly had a notebook and pen of her own. 'Did he pay for anyone else? I'm sure he paid for Mackenzie and Countess Bischkova. There's a connection between she and Etheridge. If I had to gamble, after that altercation at dinner I'd say it's the daughter...'

'Miss Marshall,' Dorward said icily, 'could I remind you that we are asking you questions? You're not interviewing us for your paper.'

Audrey pouted. 'Oh, you're no fun.'

'Tell us what else you know,' Erimem demanded.

Audrey reluctantly set her pen aside. 'Before Countess Olga started her fireworks, I'd had the most ghastly dinner with Mackenzie.'

'We saw,' Andy said. 'He thought he was very entertaining.'

Audrey grimaced at the memory. 'I'm sure he did. I was rather more interested in that horribly dull couple seated with us.'

'The Mitchells?' offered Helena.

'That's them,' Audrey confirmed. 'I kept asking questions about Etheridge just to see their reaction.'

'Why would they react?' asked Dorward.

'Daniel Mitchell is an accountant,' Audrey began.

Andy nodded. 'He looks boring enough to be one.'

'He's Etheridge's accountant,' Audrey continued. 'Not the respectable one. He's the one who handles all of Etheridge's shady dealings.'

'Really?' said Andy. 'I assume he is a busy boy.'

Audrey nodded vigorously. 'Oh, very, and he has been since just after the war. His wife is interesting, though.'

'How so?' pressed Dorward.

'They've only been married for ten months,' Audrey explained. 'She reacted every time I mentioned Etheridge.'

Dorward jotted in his notebook. 'Did she indeed?'

'She did. I've been planning to dig into that.'

'Please leave the digging to us,' said Dorward.

Audrey shook her head dismissively. 'Can't do that. I have an editor to feed.'

'One more thing,' Erimem said. 'What do you know of Professor Klimt?'

'Not much, really,' Audrey admitted. 'I made a few calls about the passengers before I boarded – I did bribe someone for an advance list of passengers. Nothing on you four, by the way. Perhaps not surprising given you're all hush-hush. Anyway, Klimt is a philosophy professor at a middling university in Germany. He's a follower of that new political bunch there. The funny little chap with the Chaplin moustache.'

'Adolf Hitler,' Andy supplied.

'That's the one.'

'Keep an eye on him,' Helena suggested. 'He's going to be trouble.'

'We had an interesting experience at dinner with Klimt,' said Dorward. 'He had a disagreement with Mr Carlisle.'

Helena *hmmed* thoughtfully. 'He's rather slid under our radar, though.'

'Your what?' asked Audrey.

'Never mind,' said Erimem. 'We will definitely have a talk

with him.'

'Miss Banks, thank you for coming.'

Penelope Banks gave Dorward a false-looking smile. 'I don't really think I had much choice, did I Sergeant? You've got sailors wandering around armed to the teeth. What's going on?'

'That's what we're trying to work out,' answered Dorward.

Penelope Banks lit a cigarette. 'I doubt if I can help you.'

'Let's see how it goes,' said Dorward. 'I suppose the first question I have to ask is why you accepted tickets on the *Agamemnon* from Lord Etheridge. You did know that he purchased the tickets?'

'You *have* been busy.'

'That's the job,' said Dorward. 'Would you answer the question please? Did you know Etheridge bought the tickets?'

'Not until I was on board and we were under way. By that time it was too late to get off. I have a high opinion of myself but walking on water is beyond even me.'

'How did you react to finding out Etheridge was responsible?' asked Erimem.

'Given your family history with him,' Dorward added.

Penelope Banks stiffened just a little, though she tried to maintain a calm appearance. 'Oh, you really have been busy bees. Yes, my father killed himself because of Etheridge and I hated the bastard for it. Pardon my language.'

'Carry on,' Andy smiled. 'Don't mind us. We call a bastard a bastard.'

'Please continue,' said Dorward.

'Etheridge broke my father and he killed himself over. What else is there to say?'

'Have you seen Etheridge since that happened?' asked Erimem.

Penelope nodded. 'Once or twice and I've called him worse than a bastard to his face.'

'I have a question,' Erimem said. 'Your father was ruined by Etheridge, but you are by all accounts very wealthy. How did you regain your wealth?'

'Hard work,' Penelope answered proudly. 'I wasn't left destitute when my father died, only in considerably reduced circumstances. However I had enough to start again, to build businesses of my own, to make my own fortune. I got lucky. I invested in the right businesses at the right time and I am now comfortable and reliant on no man for my future.'

'Which doesn't explain why Etheridge chose to get you onto this ship.' Said Helena.

'Doesn't it?' said Andy. 'We know he has history for blackmailing people... including about their private lives.'

A wry sort of wince appeared on Penelope's face, as if she had been caught in a fib. 'I heard that someone had been snooping around, asking questions. Etheridge had someone following me?'

'Actually, she was investigating Etheridge,' Dorward explained. 'You were just part of the story that came up.'

Andy added, 'She doesn't care who you love, and neither does anyone in this room.'

A look of appreciation appeared on Penelope's face. 'Etheridge was initially surprised to see me aboard, but he quickly made his move. He said he would make my... closeness with Lucy public knowledge if I didn't sell my businesses to him for a third of their worth.'

'How did you answer?' asked Dorward.

'I didn't,' Penelope replied quickly. 'I talked with Lucy. Her family is Catholic. They would disown her. We would be ruined even if the authorities chose not to act against us. I had not answered but I see no option other than to give in to his demand. I will sell to him when we return to England. I will hate myself for doing it but I will sell.'

'That won't be possible,' Erimem said. 'The offer is no longer available. Lord Etheridge was found dead a few hours ago.'

Penelope's mouth dropped open in shock. She took a moment to compose herself. 'Is it awful for me to say I am not sorry?'

'That depends if you killed him,' said Dorward.

Penelope shook her head vigorously. 'No. No, I didn't... but whoever did it has my thanks.'

'Could it have been Lucy?' asked Helena.

'Not if Etheridge was killed in the last few hours,' Penelope replied. 'We have been together all evening.'

'Alone?' asked Dorward.

'No, we're not asking what you were doing,' Andy said quickly. 'We're saying that an alibi supplied by friends is always weaker.'

Penelope smiled appreciatively. 'We were playing bridge. We were invited to play by that appallingly dull couple.'

'The Mitchells,' Helena supplied.

Penelope nodded. 'It was unbearable. We eventually lost deliberately just to make the night end.'

'Which means you were busy while someone ended Lord Etheridge's night quite brutally,' said Dorward.

Penelope pushed her chair back. 'So I can go?'

'Just one thing, said Erimem. 'Did you know that Mr Mitchell was Lord Etheridge's accountant?'

The young woman stiffened visibly. 'No. No, I didn't.'

'And if you had known?' Erimem pressed.

'We wouldn't have been playing cards last night giving him an alibi.'

'You're a crooked accountant.'

Helena replied to Dorward's statement. 'Is there any other kind?'

'My husband is not a criminal,' said Mrs Mitchell stiffly.

'He certainly works for one,' said Erimem. 'Unless you would like to deny that Lord Etheridge has been involved in some very dubious activities.'

'I don't know anything about that,' Mrs Mitchell lied very badly.

'Try again, Pinocchio,' said Andy.

Mr Mitchell placed a hand over his wife's to stop her from answering. 'I don't know what he does,' Mr Mitchell said. 'I just handled the transaction.'

'And that's in the past,' Mrs Mitchell interrupted. 'My husband has resigned from Lord Etheridge's service.'

'And when was this?' asked Dorward.

'Six weeks ago.'

'And you came on this trip as a what?' Helena asked. 'A

116

holiday to celebrate? A belated honeymoon?'

'Just a holiday,' said Mr Mitchell. 'A chance to get away, you know.'

'But not to get away from Lord Etheridge,' said Erimem pointedly.

'Well, we didn't know he was going to be aboard,' Mrs Mitchell protested.

Erimem closed the trap. 'Even though he paid for your tickets?'

'What?'

'Lord Etheridge paid for your tickets,' said Andy. 'Didn't you know?'

Mrs Mitchell rounded on her husband. 'Daniel? Daniel Mitchell, is that true? Did that man pay for these tickets?'

'Yes,' he admitted meekly.

'Why did you agree to take them? You don't work for him anymore.'

Daniel Mitchell's shoulders slumped.

'Daniel, what happened?'

'He came to see me at the hotel,' Daniel Mitchell sighed. 'He told me that I wasn't allowed to resign. If I tried to leave his employ, he would ruin me.'

'Why didn't you tell me?' his wife demanded.

'I didn't want to ruin the holiday.'

She didn't believe him. 'You just didn't want to tell me. You were afraid to.'

'I just didn't want to ruin things,' he whined.

'Well, they're ruined now,' Mrs Mitchell exploded. 'You'll see Etheridge and tell him you resign. Today.'

'He'll ruin me.'

'He won't,' said Etheridge.

Daniel Mitchell shook his head in resignation. 'You don't know him. He's ruthless.'

'He's also breathless and pulseless,' said Andy. 'We found him dead a few hours ago.'

'Who did it?' Mr Mitchell asked after a long moment.

His wife shook her head. 'Why do you think they're talking to us?'

'You think I did it?' Mr Mitchell squeaked.

'I'd say your missus is more likely,' Andy said, 'but you've got the alibi of playing bridge.'

'Lovely people,' Mrs Mitchell cooed. 'Very friendly.'

Andy didn't try to sound convinced. 'I'm sure.'

Erimem again tried to focus on the pertinent facts. 'Did you handle payments between Lord Etheridge and anyone on board the Agamemnon? At any time, not just recently.'

Mr Mitchell shifted uncomfortably in his chair. 'It's not quite that simple.'

'Feel free to explain,' said Dorward.

'Sometimes it was simply passing money to them from an untraceable account. Other times it's more complex and involves other countries and companies there.'

'Which doesn't answer whether you funnelled money to any of the people on the Agamemnon,' Erimem pointed out.

Daniel Mitchell nodded.

'Nodding's no good,' Dorward said sharply. 'Tell us who you paid.'

Daniel Mitchell was a weak man and he wilted under the harshness of the voices facing him. 'We paid Colonel Mackenzie a considerable amount of money over the years. The ship's captain and doctor as well.'

'We know that,' Erimem said sharply.

Mitchell sought a piece of information to appease his interrogators. 'Do you know that I had to send money to Professor Klimt?'

'Why?' Erimem asked. 'What did you pay him for?'

Mitchell shook his head. 'I don't know.'

She didn't believe him. 'You are lying. You stink of it.'

'Well, Mr Mitchell,' said Dorward easily, 'are you lying?'

Mitchell wilted further. 'I don't know for sure, not for certain.'

'Oh, just tell them,' his wife snapped. 'They're going to find out. That's if they don't know already.'

'Listen to her,' Erimem warned Mitchell.

Mitchell gave way under his wife's icy stare. 'Professor Klimt is an ally of the new German chancellor, Herr Hitler. There are strict rules on German rearmament.'

'We all know about the Treaty of Versailles,' Helena said.

Mitchell continued, 'Lord Etheridge owns factories... weapons factories... in various parts of the world. He is supplying weapons to Germany. Weapons they're prohibited from having.'

Dorward sat back in his chair and scrutinised the accountant. 'And you helped him?'

'He'll destroy me for talking to you.'

His wife let loose an exasperated sigh. 'They wouldn't be talking to you if they didn't already know about his activities.'

'Well, that and he's as dead as a doornail,' Andy said, sounding as if she relished giving that piece of information to people. 'We found him a few hours back.'

'Dead?' whispered Mitchell.

'Very,' Andy confirmed.

'Oh.'

'So, he can't hurt you now, can he?' said Dorward.

Erimem moved closer, her intensity was remarkably intimidating for one so petite. 'So tell us everything.'

'Etheridge uses women. Abuses them. My daughter was taken in by him. He manipulated her, lied to her, told her that he loved her. Used those lies to... to take her honour. When she found that she was... that she was pregnant, Etheridge had no interest in her, and refused to do the decent thing. And then he came to me and told me that if I didn't sell my chain of hotels to him for a fraction of the real worth he would have my daughter arrested for trying to blackmail him into marrying her when she had... dallied with his driver. None of it was true, of course. None of it. She's a good girl, my Wendy. She's just him pawn in taking my hotels.'

'Thank you, Mr Reubens.'

'Mr Hove, it's rather odd to find a noted free-thinking socialist radical travelling First Class.'

Dorward set down a sheet of paper and peered at Hove.

'Is it?' Hove answered. 'Yes, I suppose it is.'

'Could it have anything to do with the fact that Lord Etheridge paid for your ticket?' Dorward asked mildly.

Hove's reaction was noticeable. He sat bolt upright, instantly defensive. 'How do you know that? What's he told you?'

'We will ask the questions,' Erimem said, clearly enjoying her role as some kind of enforcer in the interrogations. 'You answer them.'

Andy took over. 'Starting with why the middle of son of Lord Albrighton, one of the most prominent government peers of the past twenty years became a socialist writer living under a not particularly confusing pseudonym. Albrighton and Hove? Really?'

All eyes turned to look at Andy. 'Okay. I'm impressed,' said Helena.

Andy smiled sweetly. 'I paid attention in politics class.'

Dorward offered Hove a forced smile which didn't come close to reaching his eyes. 'So tell us, Mr Hove if that's the name you prefer, what turned you red and what is your connection with Lord Etheridge?'

'I assure you that Etheridge can't harm you now,' Erimem added.

Hove's pride bristled at the suggestion he might be afraid. 'What makes you think he hurt me?'

Dorward sighed. 'He hurt everyone else he brought onto this ship. We know he paid for your ticket.'

'Oh.' Hove shrugged. 'No point in denying that, then, is there? He will ruin me, though. And my father.'

'Only if he comes back as a ghost,' said Andy.

Hove almost leaped from his seat. 'He's dead?'

Andy nodded. 'And he's not likely to get better.'

'So you can tell us,' said Erimem.

Hove sniffed and sucked his bottom lip before replying. 'I suppose I don't really have an option. All right. My father was – and still is – involved in many parts of the allocation of the nation's defence contracts. As the second son I was the spare for the heir. That meant I was free to do whatever I chose and I had the money to do it. I ran with a bad set, drank too much, womanised too much and became too fond of the poppy. Uncontrollably fond of it, to be honest. It was my own fault, really. No self-control, but Etheridge has to take more than a small share of the blame. He cultivated bad habits in us all.

Obsessions. Addictions. It gave him some control over us so that he could use us. My father cut me off financially and Etheridge kept me fed with the poison. At least until he cut me off. He had given me a lot. Now it was my turn to pay him back. All he wanted was a folder from my father's desk. I was so desperate for my drugs that I agreed, and gave him the folder. The next thing I knew was that he had undercut one of his competitors for a contract and that other company went out of business. More than a thousand jobs were lost. It crippled a community. I ruined all those lives. I left and I've never been back. I weaned myself off the filth the hard way. When I came out of it I saw things clearer. My weakness was in part responsible but Etheridge's greed, that was the real toxin. The greed of my own class. I was someone else inside when I emerged from my recovery so I literally became someone else. I travelled, I saw the world. I saw different peoples and cultures and ways of life. I saw people who thrived without our obsession with money.'

'And you became a... communist?' asked Helena.

'No, just a socialist,' Hove answered defiantly, 'and I'm comfortable being one.'

Andy raised her fist in a Wolfie Smith salute. 'Up the workers, brother. Power to the people.'

'Are you mocking me?'

'Actually, no,' Andy grinned. 'It's not like me at all, but no, I'm not.'

'As it happens I do think the workers should have more power and more money,' said Hove.

'So do I,' agreed Andy.

'I assume you are content in your life?' Erimem asked.

'I think I am, yes.'

Erimem continued, 'Then why are you returning to Britain?'

'Well, my father is dying. Stomach cancer. I don't think he has too much longer left. My brother thought it would be good if I could make peace with the old fellow before he died. Unfortunately, when I saw him on the ship yesterday, Etheridge agreed. He wanted me back in the fold to get his hooks into my brother. I told him to sod off.'

'And what did he say?' asked Erimem.

'That I could go to prison for passing on confidential

government documents,' Hove said with a resigned expression. 'However, as you can see, I am prepared to face the consequences of my actions. Sergeant, if you're going to arrest me, please do so.'

'He is not going to arrest you,' Erimem said.

That surprised Dorward. 'I'm not?'

'Though we may shoot you if you have lied at all,' Andy told Hove.

'I haven't,' Hove said earnestly. 'It actually feels rather good to get that off of my chest. Pity Etheridge is dead. I'd have liked to testify against him in court.'

'He is facing a somewhat higher justice at the moment,' said Dorward.

Andy nodded. 'I imagine he's feeling the heat from the flames already.'

Dorward indicated the door. 'Thank you, Mr Hove. You can go.'

'Doctor Griffiths? Doctor Griffiths?'

'It's no use,' Helena told Ibrahim. 'He's paralytic.'

Ibrahim agreed. 'He couldn't answer if we asked him what his name is.'

'He's got questions to answer, though.'

'They'll have to wait till he sobers up, though,' Ibrahim said.

He and Helena had come to Griffiths' quarters to tale him for questioning. They had found him lying in a stupor, reeking of stale booze.

Helena glanced at one of the sailors who had come along as their escort. 'Somebody go through this room and make sure there's no alcohol in here – of any kind. Not even medical alcohol.'

'He can't hide from our questions in booze indefinitely,' said Ibrahim.

'It's going to be much worse for him answering through a howler of a hangover.'

Ibrahim nodded. 'Good.'

CHAPTER NINE

'We have many people with reasons to kill this man and as many reasons to have him alive and explanations for where they were for when he died,' Erimem said. She was pacing the saloon, her chin down.

Andy translated. 'What my dear chum is trying to say is that we have plenty of suspects with plenty of motives and plenty of alibis,'

'I got that,' Dorward said dryly. 'Which means we have more information but we're not much further forward.'

Erimem nodded, apparently talking primarily to herself. 'And I am troubled by this one who looked like Mr Carlisle but who could not have been him.'

'Really?' Andy's eyebrows lifted. 'I'm more worried about a homicidal thumb-munching giant who seems to be world class at hide and seek.'

'I had not forgotten that.'

Andy smiled. 'Didn't think you had, love.'

'I'm concerned by all of it,' Dorward sighed. He stifled a yawn.

'You need rest,' Nadia Bakshi said to him.

'I'm fine,' Dorward replied automatically.

'No, you are not,' Nadia answered. 'You are tired.'

Dorward sighed and stretched his back. 'This time out recovering has made me soft. I can usually stay up for days when I'm working.'

'You haven't eaten,' Nadia said. 'I will get you something.'

'No.' Dorward caught her arm lightly. 'Phone and have them

bring something up. I'm not having you wandering the corridors alone.'

'The corridors are full of armed sailors,' Nadia reminded him gently.

'Good,' Dorward said severely. 'That means the stewards will be safe when they bring some food up.'

Nadia sighed extravagantly. 'You are a stubborn man.'

'I'm glad somebody noticed.'

Andy had noticed movement through the small glass window in the door. 'Captain Hawkins is waiting outside.'

That made up Dorward's mind. 'We'll see him then eat.'

Andy opened the door and beckoned Captain Hawkins and a young officer into the room. 'Come on in, Captain Hawkins.'

Hawkins stood awkwardly to attention in front of the table, where Dorward still sat.

'I assume that I am no longer master of this vessel?' Captain Hawkins said to Dorward.

Dorward sighed. His eye had turned momentarily to a particularly excellent Scotch on the gantry in the bar but he knew that was off limits while he was on duty. 'With Mr Carlisle dead, who is there to take over as acting captain?'

Hawkins nudged Lieutenant Mills, who stood uncomfortably as his captain's side. 'We have a number of young lieutenants, but none of them experienced.'

Dorward's lips pursed in thought. 'Then I suppose it would be stupid to stand you down when the ship still needs run.'

'Thank you.'

Dorward raised a hand to cut off the thanks. 'But you'll come to me or my colleagues regarding anything major to do with the ship. That includes changing crew rotations, course alterations, that kind of thing.'

'I understand,' Hawkins agreed. 'We won't be changing course. We're still en route to Southampton.'

Young Lieutenant Mills shuffled uncomfortably at his captain's side. 'Begging your pardon, sir, we're not.'

Hawkins rounded on the lad. 'What do you mean? I didn't give any order to change course.'

'No, sir, Mr Carlisle did.' Mills shook his head, trying to get the words right. 'Except that's the Mr Carlisle who wasn't actually Mr Carlisle. That's what he did when he went to the bridge.'

'Well, where the devil are we going?' Hawkins demanded.

'I can't actually say without a chart, sir,' Mills answered.

Hawkins turned to Dorward. 'We'd better see to this on the bridge.'

'Do you want to go to this bridge?' Erimem asked Dorward.

'No,' Dorward answered, 'but I'll go anyway.'

Erimem nodded. 'I will go with you.'

Andy lifted herself from her chair. 'You want me to stay put?'

Erimem nodded. 'In case Helena and Ibrahim come back, yes please.'

Andy grinned. 'Okay, Your Majesty.'

'You should call me that more.'

'Yeah, let me think about that... no. I will order you food though.'

This time it was Erimem who grinned. 'Thank you. I am hungry.'

The walk from the lounge to the bridge took considerably longer than it might. Forward pushed himself as fast as he could but the long day was clearly wearing him down.

Banting, a neatly bearded sailor with an obvious dislike for Lieutenant Mills was the ranking sailor on the bridge.'

'Of course I remember Mr Carlisle coming is, sir,' he answered Dorward's question. 'He relieved Mr Mills and sent his for his supper.' He managed to make the act sound like a parent dismissing a child to bed. 'After that, Mr Carlisle went around the bridge inspecting things for a few minutes.'

'Did he say anything?' Dorward asked. 'Did he engage ion a conversation with anyone?'

'No, sir,' replied Banting. 'Everything was as it should be. Then after five minutes or so, Mr Carlisle gave us a new heading. He waited until we had changed course and then disappeared. Is it true he's dead? That must be the last thing he did before he died.'

'No,' Erimem said, looking at the controls with fascination.

'It was something he did long after he died.'

Dorward nudged Hawkins. 'Can we see where that heading takes us?'

Captain Hawkins led his party to a table containing a map of Europe and North Africa. 'Here's the map. We're currently... Mills?'

The young lieutenant looked at a few readings then pointed to a spot on the map. 'We're here, sir. Our route will take us this way.' His finger trailed along the surface of the map.

'Is there anything significant on that route?' asked Erimem.

'In what way?' asked Hawkins.

'Legends,' Erimem answered. 'Stories. Lost ships. Unusual weather. Anything like that.'

Hawkins shook his head. 'Not that I know of and I've been sailing these waters since before the Great War.'

'Is this on regular shipping routes?' asked Dorward.

'Not for cruise ships,' Hawkins replied. 'We tend to stop at ports like... here and here. It could be used by cargo ships though.'

'Or pirates?' Erimem asked.

'Pirates?' Dorward choked. 'In this day and...' the scornful remark died as he saw the serious look in Captain Hawkins' face. 'You mean there really still are pirates today?'

Hawkins nodded. 'They're usually in the Atlantic and go for cargo ships, though. I don't remember them ever going for a cruise ship. Too many crew, too big to subdue.'

'So that is unlikely to be the reason,' Erimem said. 'But if I learned anything from my teacher about war, it is that if an enemy wants to get you to a place...'

'Be somewhere else,' Dorward finished for her. 'You're right.' He turned to Hawkins. 'Change course, Captain. Put us back on our heading to Southampton.'

Hawkins accepted the instruction with relief and relayed it to Banting, who acknowledged and set about altering the ship's course.

'There will be a reaction to this,' Erimem said. 'When the untrue Carlisle finds that we have changed course, he will have to act.'

Dorward agreed. 'He could try to change course again.'

'I'll ensure that course corrections can only be ordered by me,' Hawkins said. 'Or you,' he added uncomfortably to Dorward.

'When will he know we have changed course?' Erimem asked.

Hawkins' finger came down on a small mark on the map. 'Just after dawn tomorrow. When he sees that island he'll know we're not where he expects to be.'

Dorward rubbed the back of his neck, as he often seemed to do when thinking. 'What do you think?' he asked Erimem. 'Is he likely to keep his head down or try to force the issue and get back to his own course?'

'He has been bold so far,' Erimem answered. 'He has been careful to avoid being found but he has come into the open when it has been necessary and he has killed without mercy. The change in course was important enough for him to risk exposure. I think he will act quickly when he knows we are not where he wants to be.'

Dorward agreed. 'Then we'd better get ready for that.'

'I'll keep the lads on armed patrol,' Hawkins said nervously.

'Have this place guarded by armed men,' Erimem added. 'Do not let him change our direction.'

Hawkins agreed again. He appeared relieved that while he still had nominal command of the ship, the more difficult decisions were now out of his hands. 'Two inside the bridge and two outside on the door,' he agreed.

'Sounds sensible,' Dorward approved.

'Now we should eat and sleep,' Erimem said. 'If we are to face our enemy in the morning we should do it rested.

'You're right. I could really use some sleep.'

'We can't share a room,' Dorward protested to the group gathered in the small saloon. 'It's not decent.'

'We're not suggesting you get married before bedtime,' Andy protested, 'just that you sleep in the same room so you can keep each other safe. We've advised everybody else to sleep in at least pairs. You did it before.'

'That was different,' Dorward said. 'I was drugged and

unconscious.'

Nadia Bakshi placed a hand on Dorward's arm to placate him. 'It's all right. I am safe with you. I trust you to be an honourable man.'

Dorward scowled. 'You might be surprised.'

Nadia smiled confidently. 'I think not. I will be fine. Your couch is comfortable enough.'

'I suppose I'm going to find out about how comfy that couch is,' Dorward muttered. 'My mother would skelp my lug if I let a lassie take the couch while I had the bed.'

Heading towards his cabin with two armed soldiers following close behind, Captain Oscar Hawkins knew he was finished.

There had been three murders on his ship, including one of the richest and most powerful men in England. Two of his crew were dead and his part in a lucrative smuggling operation had been uncovered. It didn't matter that he had been encouraged into the smuggling by his superiors. They would deny all knowledge and hang him out to dry... but if he kept quiet he would receive a comfortable under-the-table payment that would see him through retirement... when he came out of prison.

Prison did not appeal to Hawkins one bit. He was not what he would call a tough man, and he was fond of his comforts. The idea of being incarcerated frightened him. He would face a good eighteen months to two year in jail. However, the idea of thirty years in poverty frightened him considerably more. He would endure his penance in prison to buy his comfortable retirement, preferably in a small village where stories of the sea were of no interest to anyone.

Perhaps he could appear to be helpful to the policeman, Dorward. Hand in a couple of minor figures in the smuggling operation, or something like that. The line wouldn't want any major figures in the smuggling ring unveiled but he could certainly hand over the stewards who were in on it. They would keep quiet for the promise of money at the end of it, and their sentences would be minor given how low down in the chain they were. Yes, his number might be up, but Hawkins was sure he could wangle himself an escape from the worst of it. He might even wind up retiring earlier than he might if he saw out his contract.

He arrived back at his cabin and dismissed his guard, instructing them to stand ready to meet him in the morning.

Slipping into his cabin, Hawkins began composing the message he would send to the line's office, using code to warn them of what was happening. Yes, he might just get out of this heroically in the eyes of his superiors.

Turning on the cabin's light, Hawkins only had a fraction of a second to register that he really was finished.

Lieutenant Arthur Mills was, in an odd way, relishing his new responsibilities. Whether they liked it or not, the crew had been forced to accept the he was the acting First Officer. The muttered comments and bad attitude aimed at him had disappeared from the men. Mr Carlisle's death was undoubtedly a tragedy but there was no reason to not make the most of it, was there? He could get himself a promotion and possibly even a transfer to a better ship out of this.

Puffed with pride at his new position and the respect it gave him, Mills was disappointed to see a familiar figure opening the door to the bridge.

'Did you spot anything missing from your porthole this morning?' Andy asked.

She and Erimem has just joined Ibrahim and Helena in the small corridor between their rooms.

'There's not much *double* about your *entendres* is there?' Ibrahim asked.

'There's no sign of an island anywhere near us either,' Erimem interrupted.

They made their way to Dorward's cabin and knocked gently. A bleary-eyed Nadia Bakshi answered. 'Already?' she asked, stepping aside to invite them in. There was no sign of Dorward but sounds of movement came from the small bathroom. Nadia was already dressed and Dorward emerged a few minutes later, walking with the aid of a single stick.

'I never got the hang of the early shift,' he said in greeting.

Erimem bypassed the morning pleasantries. 'We should be able to see the island outside but we can't.'

Dorward's brow furrowed. 'The sun's only just starting to rise. Maybe it's still dark...' His voice tailed off when he saw the expressions on the faces around him. 'Right. So something's not as it should be.'

'We should find Captain Hawkins,' Erimem said.

Dorward nodded. 'Could things not wait till after breakfast to go to hell?' he muttered.

Erimem's party bumped into Lieutenant Mills as they climbed the stairs towards the bridge's deck.

'Captain Hawkins?' Mills frowned. 'Yes,' he's below in the Engine Room. Something to do with the engines running slow. We're not making the speed we should.'

Andy grunted. 'That explains why there's no island in sight. That actually could be to our advantage.'

Erimem seemed unconvinced. 'Perhaps. We should find out from Hawkins when the engines will be at full power again.'

'Do you want to see him before or after breakfast?' Mills asked. 'We knew you would be early so we have a full breakfast spread ready for you below.'

'Don't mention food,' Andy moaned. 'We spent so much time running about yesterday we hardly had time to eat.'

'I will go to the Engine Room,' Erimem said. She glanced at Mills. 'If you will take me there.'

Mills nodded. 'Of course, miss. It's a bit of a rabbit warren down there. I occasionally get lost in there myself.' A shy smile appeared on the young man's. 'I'd appreciate it if you didn't mention that to anybody. I'm supposed to be acting First Officer. I should be able to know my way about the ship.'

'Your secret is safe,' Andy promised, 'as long as you feed us.' She glanced at Erimem. 'Want me to come with?'

'No, I would like you to save some breakfast for me. Fresh fruit...'

'And bacon,' Andy said comfortably, 'lots of bacon, just before it goes crispy.'

'Now you are making me hungry.' Erimem turned quickly. 'Lead on, please, Lieutenant Mills.'

'She's definitely in the mood for bacon,' Andy muttered to Helena. 'She's going at a hell of a gallop.'

Andy was right. Erimem was a good head shorter than Mills but the sailor was having to hurry to keep up.

'Better save her some bacon, then,' Helena said. She led the way towards the stairs down to the dining saloon. 'That's a kind of angry you don't want to see.'

Erimem had dropped back to Mills' shoulder as they had reached the lower levels of the ship. The young sailor led the way down the decks through corridors and passageways. Every now and then he glanced to take his bearing before moving on.

She had tried to engage Mills in conversation but he had been reluctant to answer fully. Eventually he answered. 'Captain Hawkins is in trouble. We can see that. We don't know how to react to all of you because of that. He's our captain.'

Erimem accepted the explanation and fell into the silence, following the sailor along the passage.

Breakfast was set up as a buffet. Ibrahim and Helena had joined Andy in casting aside any hint of eating healthily.

Ibrahim lifted a rasher of bacon on his fork. 'I realise this probably doesn't hit any of the health and safety standards we're used to but I don't care. I love bacon.'

'Bacon broke me,' Andy admitted. 'I was vegetarian when I started work in the canteen. Somewhere around the thousandth bacon roll, I caved. My morals and my taste buds are still arguing over it.'

A steward hurried over, looking agitated. 'I have a message from one of the cabin stewards. He sounded... well, he sounded terrified. He asked for you to go to the Captain's cabin immediately.'

Andy stuffed the rasher of bacon into her mouth. 'Bugger,' she said.

* * *

It took the around five minutes to reach the Captain's cabin. Dorward, rested and fed, was able to keep up far better than he had the previous night.

A terrified steward was standing outside of the closed door. 'In there,' he said. 'I wouldn't,' he warned, 'not the ladies. They shouldn't see this.'

'Rubbish,' Andy snorted. 'We don't need protecting, you know.' She pushed the door open and stopped in the doorway. 'I dunno, though. Kind of glad I didn't have breakfast now.'

'What is it?' Helena asked. She eased past Andy into the room. 'Oh, shit.'

'Christ,' Dorward breathed.

The remains of two bodies were scattered around the room. Blood had sprayed the walls and formed in pools around the various body parts.

Helena quickly set about making what examination she could. 'It's Captain Hawkins,' she said. 'His neck has been crushed. I'd guess from a single blow. He would have been dead instantly.' She moved to the second body, lifting an arm to look at the rough and ragged edges of skin. 'This one's been torn apart,' she said. 'I mean literally torn apart. The skin is ripped not cut. The bones have been pulled apart. This was frenzied, wild.'

'Shit,' Andy breathed. She had gingerly turned the dismembered head. Wide eyes stared out of a familiar face. 'That's Mills,' she said, 'the lieutenant who took Erimem to find the captain.'

'This blood is congealing,' Helena said. 'He's been dead for hours.'

'So who was that with Erimem?' Dorward asked.

Helena, Andy and Ibrahim didn't answer. They were already running out of the door.

'I am beginning to think I should have had breakfast before coming to see the Captain,' Erimem said.

'It's a big ship,' Mills answered.

'And I take your point about it being easy to get lost in,' Erimem mused. She had stopped by a set of signs on the wall. 'I am no expert but I know the Engine Room is to the back of the ship and you have now passed three signs which tell us we are moving forward.' Her eyebrow arched quizzically. 'Can you explain that?'

Mills waited just a fraction of a second too long to answer. 'The Engine Room is very large on a ship this size. The door...' his voice trailed off and a sly smile crept across his lips. 'You won't believe anything I tell you now, will you? You are too suspicious of me.'

'I am suspicious of everyone.' Erimem took a short step backwards. 'Is there a reason I should be suspicious of you?'

'No,' Mills answered. His face seemed to ripple as if it was becoming liquid. The skin roiled and moved around his face, becoming misshapen and changing colour. The nose stretched outwards and the mouth morphed up until it joined the nose on a sort of beak. The skin was darkening to red with scales growing out of it. Mills' eyes were gone, replaced by reptilian eyes on either side of a hairless head which seemed to have doubled in size. Mills himself has grown, stretching a metre taller and muscles bulging inside his clothes before tearing free of the flesh. The arms and legs grew, showing extra joints above the arms and wrists. It took less than ten seconds for the quiet Lieutenant Mills to become this scarlet demon. Its leathery lips pulled back to show long, sharp teeth.

You remind me of Drofen,' Erimem said, surprised by how little her voice shook. 'I wonder if you are related.'

The creature stopped, its head tilted in curiosity. She had surprised it by mentioning a relatively obscure race of carrion feeders from a distant world halfway across the galaxy. The surprise didn't last long. The creature sprang forward, long clawed fingers reaching for Erimem. The delay had been enough time for her to take another step backwards. Heaving with all her strength she slid a safety door across. The creature slammed into the heavy metal door. She could hear its claws scrabbling for some kind of purchase on the other side. It was solid and heavy. Erimem guessed that the door had been designed to hold back either fire or water flooding the ship. The dents appearing from the beat's blows showed that it would not hold this creature at bay for long. For once, the wise course of action was to retreat. She turned and ran back along the corridor. The door behind shook under more impacts and she heard the horrific sound of metal tearing. She risked a look back. The creature that had so recently looked like Lieutenant Mills was tearing and pushing its way through the torn metal of the door.

She wasn't going to make it to safety in time. The creature would certainly catch up with her. There had to be something...

Something...

Yes, there was one weapon...

Erimem forced herself to run faster, turning hard left and bolting up the stairs ahead.

There were clawing, slapping footsteps behind.

Don't look back.

She kept running.

Up the stairs. Turn right. Keep running. Another set of stairs. Keep running.

The footsteps behind were closer. She heard the breathing.

Ignore it.

Keep running.

She bolted up the stairs, turned right. There was a glass cabinet ahead. She tore it open and yanked out the heavy axe which had been clipped under the word EMERGENCY. She dropped back towards the next set of steps but she knew she wouldn't get up them in time. The footsteps behind were too close.

Erimem stopped and turned, the axe raised, ready to swing. The creature was five metres behind her. Its talons flexed and it moved slowly forward. She pushed her fear down and inspected the beast carefully. Its leathery skin looked tough. Could she rip deep enough with the axe to do it real damage? Its skull looked solid and heavy but perhaps if she could get its face or eyes... no, her best chance was to hack through its limbs. If she could cut through a leg at a weak point the creature would be off balance and she could attack and find another weak spot.

The creature sprang at Erimem. She dropped low and swung her axe hard. It caught the creature in the left leg just below the knee, breaking the skin. The creature screamed in pain and jerked its leg, yanking the axe from Erimem's grasp. It clattered away along the corridor.

She had to get the axe back.

The creature turned and screamed in rage.

The axe was too far away.

If she could get through the door behind her there could be something in there she could use.

'Erimem, get down!'

She recognised the voice and trusted Andy completely. She dropped to the deck. A moment later two gunshots exploded in the enclosed passageway. The creature screamed. Two more gunshots roared and she was aware of the creature running past her, hurrying away along the corridor. She was on her feet quickly and found herself surrounded by her friends.

'Are you hurt?' Helena demanded, looking for any sign of injury.

Erimem shook her head and was grabbed into a hug first by Andy and then Ibrahim. 'I am not hurt, but only because you got here.'

'What the hell was that thing?' Helena demanded.

'It looked Auld Nick himsel',' Dorward said. He gave Erimem a curt nod. 'I'm glad you're all right.' He looked back at two nervous sailors holding rifles. 'You two keep your eyes peeled. If you see that thing again, shoot it.'

The two men blanched at the thought of seeing the demonic beast again.

'What was it?' Helena repeated. 'I'm glad you're okay, by the way.'

'Thank you.' Erimem took a few step along the corridor and dropped to a knee to look at the pool of deep purple blood on the deck. 'That was Lieutenant Mills. I know it sounds impossible but I watched him change from Mills to that creature in just seconds.'

'We believe you,' Ibrahim said. 'The real Mills is in pieces up in the Captain's cabin.'

'We don't mean "in pieces" as in he's crying or anything,' Andy said. 'He's actually torn into little pieces. That's how we knew your Mills was a phoney.'

'But we didn't know he was a shape-shifter.' Ibrahim

shrugged as Andy and Helena gave him a puzzled look. 'Hey, I've seen *Star Trek*, I speak geek sometimes.'

'What now?' Andy asked.

'Get everybody together,' Dorward said. 'Gather them in the Dining Room so we can keep them safe.'

'And then?' Ibrahim asked.

Erimem had picked up her axe. She sniffed at the odd-smelling purple blood. 'And then we hunt this beast.'

The First Class passengers aboard the *Agamemnon* complained loudly at being dragged from their beds early. Several demanded to see Captain Hawkins to complain.

'You're out of luck unless you've got a medium with you,' Andy answered. 'Now everybody sit down.'

Colonel Mackenzie was among the most vociferous complainants. 'What the devil is all that talk of a medium?'

'Captain Hawkins is dead,' Erimem said flatly. 'He was murdered by a beast which is loose on this ship. You have been gathered here because this is the best place for us to keep you safe.'

'Safe?' Mackenzie snorted. 'I don't need some chit of a darkie foreign girl keeping me safe. I'm going out there to see what's going on.'

Mackenzie tried to move around Erimem. She moved quickly, caught his arm and twisted. A moment later the Colonel was staggering backwards until the backs of his knees hit a chair and he dropped into it. He stared in shocked and embarrassment. His fists clenched at his side and he started to push himself up.

Dorward stepped between the soldier and Erimem. 'Stay where you are, Colonel Mackenzie.'

'Damn it! I'm ranking officer now.'

'And you are a smuggler with reason to hate Etheridge,' Erimem snapped. 'If you try to leave again, I will knock you down again.'

Mackenzie glared but said nothing.

Helena drew her party closer and spoke quietly. 'Maybe we should fill them all in what's been happening.'

Nadia Bakshi surprised everyone, herself included, by being

first to answer. 'You think we should tell a room of people that there is a monster on the ship killing people?'

Andy agreed. 'Mentioning the alien might not be the wisest course of action. We should keep that bit quiet.'

'Alien?' Dorward looked as if he had been punched. 'Nobody mentioned alien to me.'

'Have you ever seen a shape-shifting creature like that on Earth?' Erimem asked patiently. 'Or even heard of one?'

'No,' Dorward admitted, 'but I'd never heard of women in the Intelligence Service either and here you lot are.'

'Then trust our intelligence,' Helena said with a humourless smile. 'Buggerlugs is alien.'

Dorward took a moment and looked to Nadia for support. Eventually he sighed. 'All right – but I'm damned if I'm writing the report for this.'

'Okay,' Helena said. 'Let's get on with it. Who wants to do the honours?'

Erimem's shoulders slumped as five pairs of eyes turned to her. 'Why me?'

'You're royalty,' Andy said, 'you're trained for this.'

'I'm trained at telling people what to do,' Erimem grumbled mutinously, but she moved towards the waiting passengers, who had all thankfully slumped into seats. 'The problem is that people aren't trained to actually do as I tell them.' She raised her hands to quiet the conversation. 'If you will be quiet we will tell you what has happened, at least as much as we know.'

The low rumble died.

'All right,' Mackenzie said. 'Tell us.'

Erimem glared at the soldier for a second before continuing. 'We have discovered that many of you knew Etheridge before coming aboard this ship. Some of you have worked with him illegal activities, others have suffered badly at his hands.' She paused. 'In fact, even those who were his allies have also been his victims. He was a vicious man who found your weaknesses and used them against you. He used blackmail to coerce many of you into working for him. Which raises a question... why did he bring you all onto this ship?' She paused and looked around the assembled faces. 'Did he bring you here to taunt you? Did he bring you here to show that he could control you? If he did, why was he surprised to see so many of you? Does that mean that one of you – or all of you – had come together to find justice or perhaps revenge against this man who had wronged you?'

'Poppycock!' snapped Mackenzie.

Helena took over from Erimem. 'Is it?' she asked. 'You have blood on your hands for the death of a woman and your unborn child. Etheridge used that to make you smuggle for him. That is going to cost you the military career you hold so dearly.'

'That is only an accusation,' Mackenzie said sharply. 'Nothing has been proven.'

'*Yet*,' Helena added. 'So Colonel Mackenzie had reason to hate Etheridge.' She turned to Countess Olga Bischkova. 'And so did Countess Bischkova. Etheridge mistreated her family after the Revolution.'

Countess Bischkova was irritated by being suggested as a suspect by offered the smallest bob of the head in acknowledgement of the delicate manner in which her situation had been presented.

Dorward picked up the discussion. 'Mr Reubens and Mr Hove also both have reasons to despise Lord Etheridge and to see revenge against him. As indeed do Miss Banks, Miss Isaac and the Mitchells.' He nodded at the bleary-looking Doctor Griffiths. 'The ship's medic, Dr Griffiths has had dealings with Lord Etheridge, too.' He looked around the room. The Agamemnon's surgeon looked back through bleary eyes. 'Which mean that there are at least ten of you aboard who had a reason to kill Lord Etheridge.'

'And one of you here planned to kill the pig Etheridge,' Erimem said. 'The fact that you all knew Etheridge is important, as is the fact that you had a grudge against him. It is also important that Etheridge paid for your passage aboard this ship.'

'At least Etheridge's bank account paid for the tickets,' Andy said, holding up the chequebook. 'You see, most of the time Etheridge seems to have had his accountant issue cheques. The cheques here... the writing on the stubs is a pretty good copy of Etheridge...' she passed the narrative back to Erimem.

'...But you have had a great deal of practice at copying your master's name, have you not, Mr Anderson?' Erimem's eyes turned to Warren Anderson.

The valet blanched. 'I...'

'Will really regret it if you lie to her,' Ibrahim said quietly. 'Just thought you should know that.'

Anderson swallowed hard but said nothing.

Erimem continued her interrogation. 'Tell us, Mr Anderson, did you plan to kill Lord Etheridge and then expect one of these passengers to take the blame?'

'Or,' Andy interjected, 'have you gone all *Murder on the Orient Express* and is everyone involved in a plan to murder Etheridge?'

'I didn't kill him,' Anderson blurted in protest.

'We know,' Erimem said, 'but we are trying to work out what you *planned* to do.'

Anderson ignored the question. 'You know I didn't kill him?'

'Of course,' Andy said sourly. 'You're far too wimpy and puny to kill Etheridge the way he was done in. Besides, we've seen the... well, the culprit.'

'Then why are we here?' Mackenzie protested. 'Get out there and catch the scoundrel.'

Andy humphed. 'You wouldn't say that if you had seen the bugger.'

Erimem interrupted. 'That does not answer the question of what your plan was, Mr Anderson.'

'I knew nothing of any plan,' objected Countess Bischkova.

'Neither did I,' added Hove.

Others also shook their head and protested their innocence.

'Looks like you were acting alone,' Dorward said. 'What a bad lad.'

'Wait a minute,' protested Anderson. 'You said you know I didn't kill Lord Etheridge. You can't arrest me for something I didn't do.'

'Perfectly true,' Dorward agreed, 'but I can lift you for forging cheques to buy these tickets and for planning to implicate people in a murder.'

'Why?' asked Ibrahim. 'Why did you want to kill the man who paid you?'

'You met him, didn't you?' Anderson answered.

Ibrahim looked unimpressed. Helena was, too. 'You can do better than that,' she said.

Dorward agreed. 'You heard her. Try again.'

Anderson sighed. 'It was a woman. It was always a woman. He liked using them, either for his own pleasure or as a way to get people to do what he wanted. He got a thrill from using and controlling them. He was an animal and he deserved to die.' His chin jutted forward defiantly. 'And I wish to God that I had killed him for the way he used my niece. She's never recovered from how he... from what he did.'

'And you still worked for him?' asked Andy.

'I couldn't get revenge otherwise,' Anderson replied, 'and I couldn't have used his knowledge to trade my way to a fortune on the stock market if I left either. My niece may never trust another human being as long as she lives but at least she'll be wealthy.'

Erimem nodded slowly and spoke up. 'There you have the reason why you are all here. Etheridge was a brute and he hurt you all.' She paused. 'All of that is true but there is another reason we have brought you all here. Etheridge's killer – the killer of Mr Carlisle, the unfortunate serving girl, the captain and Mr Mills... the killer has a talent for disguise.'

'But it seems to have a need for the ship to steer a certain course,' Dorward took over. 'We tracked its blood trail to First Class but couldn't narrow it any further.'

Ibrahim opened the door and waved six armed sailors into the Dining Room.

'While you were here,' Erimem said, 'we had every First Class cabin searched. There was no sign of the killer, which means it is among us here somewhere.'

A disturbed rumble of conversation started among the passengers.

'Why do you call the killer "it", for heaven's sake?' demanded Mackenzie.

'If you are unlucky you will see,' Erimem replied.

Dorward spoke again. 'The killer wants to pass through a certain part of the sea. I'm afraid that's not going to happen. We have diverted course and will make port this afternoon. Until then I'm afraid everyone is going to have to remain in the room.'

'Where one of us is a killer?' Countess Bischkova objected.

'These men will keep us safe,' Dorward assured her.

Erimem nodded. 'And when we reach port, the authorities there will uncover the truth and deal with it. Until then we will all stay here in this room.'

Dorward smacked the handle of his stick down on a table to quiet the protests. 'I realise that won't be popular or enjoyable, but that's how it's going to be. Anyone who doesn't like that decision can make an official complaint after we reach port.

Support came from an unexpected source. 'It sounds eminently sensible,' said Colonel Mackenzie. 'Keep the enemy at bay until he can be subdued.'

Countess Bischkova was less impressed. 'Even if they are in this room?'

'I doubt if anyone can survive six good men with rifles,' Mackenzie answered.

'Refreshments will be brought in a while,' Dorward said. 'Until then, just make yourselves as comfortable as you can.'

Doctor Griffiths forced himself up onto his feet. He looked unsteady and hungover. 'What do you want me to do?' he asked.

'Just sit down and wait,' Erimem answered.

Griffiths frowned uncertainly. 'I'm not a passenger. I'm part of the crew. I have duties.'

'Who will you report to?' Andy asked. 'Pretty much every senior member of the crew is dead and your patients are here.'

'There must be something useful I can do,' Griffiths protested, shambling past the armed sailors towards Dorward.

'Just sit down,' Dorward repeated. 'It'll give you time to sober up.'

Erimem's head tilted suspiciously. 'Where were you when the sailors found you?' she asked Griffiths.

'Well, I wes...'

Erimem didn't let him finish. 'Andy, where was the creature hit when it was shot?'

'Leg and arms,' Andy replied. 'Why...' her eyes turned to Griffiths and immediately saw what Erimem was alluding to... the way Griffiths limped on one leg and the way he carried an arm... 'Oh, shit.'

Griffiths changed in seconds. His body stretched, the skin darkened becoming red and inhuman. Fingers grew into talons and the face was pulled out into that monstrous beak.

The sailors panicked. Two managed to raise their rifles. One of them fired wildly but the other had the weapon ripped from his hands and was sent sprawling as the butt of the weapon was smashed against his jaw, sending him reeling into Dorward, who collapsed under the man's weight.

The creature's eyes turned to the door. Nearest to its escape stood Nadia Bakshi, who had stayed back to take notes of everything being said. The beast raised a clawed hand to strike her down. Its claws began to swish down... but then the creature collapsed, landing hard on its face.

Erimem stood behind it, Dorward's stick in her hand. She had used the curved handle to hook the creature's ankle and bring it down. As it began to right itself she swung the stick again, this time into the beast's face. Purple blood sprayed the gleaming white wall. She twisted the stick and swung at the head again. This time the curved handle found the creature's eye and it screamed in pain Blood and a clear viscous fluid oozed from the damaged eye. The walking stick came down again but this time the creature was waiting. It swatted the stick from Erimem's hands, shattering it with one violent movement.

Erimem ignored the loss of her weapon. Her hands were already at her back, drawing the two carving knives she had taken from the galley.

The creature reared up to strike at her...

A rifle's shot sounded like an explosion by her ear.

Dorward had picked up a fallen rifle and fired into the beast's hide. A moment later he fired again. The creature roared. Spurred on by Dorward, the sailors recovered their composure and fired.

Outnumbered and unable to win, the creature smashed its way through the door leaving smears of purple blood in its wake.

'What the devil was that thing?' Mackenzie exclaimed.

'That was the killer,' Dorward answered.

'And thanks for your help,' Andy snapped sourly. 'Well done to the big, brave soldier.'

'It was the Devil,' Olga Bischkova said. 'A demon.'

'We'll explain later,' Andy shouted, hurrying after Erimem who was already halfway through the door in pursuit of the creature.

Dorward struggled to follow but was halted by Ibrahim.

'We'll get this. You get the hard bit – looking after the public.'

Dorward's shoulders slumped. 'I'm in no state to chase after it.'

'Ibrahim, come on,' Helena called from the door. 'You four,' she shouted at the armed sailors. 'Follow us.'

Dorward nodded his approval at the sailors, though they were already hurrying out after Ibrahim and Helena.

'Sit.' Nadia had brought a chair to Dorward's side and he gratefully slumped into it.

'Are you hurt?' he asked.

Her black hair swished as she shook her head. 'I am fine, thanks to you and Erimem.'

'Mostly Erimem.'

'Perhaps,' Nadia said quietly, 'but I like you a good deal more than her. Does it shock you that a woman should be so forward?'

'Only that she would be so forward with me. I'm nothing special.'

Nadia Bakshi brushed a stray hair from over Dorward's eyes. 'You will forgive me if I disagree.'

CHAPTER TEN

The creature's destination very quickly became obvious to the party following it.

'It's heading for the bridge,' Andy shouted.

'Obviously,' Erimem agreed.

'Can we warn the crew up there?'

'I doubt it.'

Helena was close behind them. 'Just keep moving.'

There was chaos on the bridge. Two bloodied members of the crew staggered along the corridor away from the bridge. A third was still in the control room but clearly dying from the wounds gouged across his face and chest. The creature dropped to its knees, pressing its claws to the sailor's throat to stop Erimem's party from coming closer.

Slowly, the creature lifted the dying sailor's hand to his mouth.

'Don't!' Helena yelled, but the creature ignored her.

The sailor screamed as the creature bit into the hand. When its mouth cleared away, everything from the palm down was gone.

The creature tilted its head back and swallowed. A moment later its flesh boiled and lightened. The body seemed to shrink becoming more human in dimensions. A few moments later, a copy of the wounded sailor on the floor, who had slipped into some kind of shocked state.

'If you come closer, I will kill him.' The transformed creature spoke uncomfortably as it learned to speak with a new mouth.

'If we don't get him to the surgery he'll die anyway,' Helena retorted.

Erimem's attention was not on the dying sailor. She was only interested in her enemy. 'That is why you consume part of your victim. That is how you come to look like them.'

'DNA is absorbed through digestion, along with some access to memories.' The alien's head tilted as if he was working on a puzzle. 'You are not as surprised as the others on this vessel. You mentioned our Drofen cousins. You are more advanced than the rest.'

'Compliments will get you nowhere,' Helena said sharply.

Erimem tried to take control of the conversation again. 'What is in the water that you have needed to alter the course of the ship twice?'

'Three times,' the alien answered. 'Although you changed course too late second time. The beacon was already activated.'

'Meaning?' Erimem demanded.

The *Agamemnon* shook.

'You've got to be shitting me.' Andy pointed to the waters ahead of the liner. The calm surface has begun to bubble and roil. The sea was thrashed to a foam as something huge and metallic pushed its way to the surface. 'An alien submarine?' She shook her head. Part of the angular ship's hull was now visible and showed a vicious gash around ten metres in length in its side. 'Or a damaged spaceship.'

'Is that why you brought this ship here?' Erimem asked. 'To repair your own?'

'And to use for parts in repairing my ship,' the alien said. 'The ship is primitive but I can adapt pieces to allow for a flight back to the mothership.'

'Mothership?' Andy asked. 'Why do I not like the sound of that?'

'How many more of you are there?' Helena said. 'How many more are out there in your mothership?'

'Enough.'

Erimem's back straightened. 'Enough to invade? To conquer?'

The alien's only reply was to laugh.

Erimem took a step closer to the alien. 'I do not think we will let you repair your ship today or invade this world.'

'And how will you stop me? With my crew I will kill you all and devour you slowly.'

Erimem's lifted her chin defiantly. 'You say your ship needs this vessel?' Her hand reached out and pushed the *Agamemnon* up to maximum speed. 'Have it!'

The Agamemnon lurched slightly as its engines increased their efforts and the liner picked up speed. It cut through the waves accelerating towards the recently surfaced spaceship. The alien screamed in protest but he was too late. The Agamemnon's bow ploughed into the damaged hull of the alien craft, sinking itself deep into the enemy ship. Metal screeched as the water pulled the ships apart. Klaxons wailed on the Agamemnon and a high pitched alarm howled from the alien vessel. Whatever defences had been holding the water at bay on the aliens craft had been breached by the prow of the liner and water was pouring into the craft making it list alarmingly.

The alien, still in the form of the sailor, screamed in rage and was only stopped from attacking Erimem by the muzzles of the rifles aimed at it.

'You can die here alone or die with your own people,' Erimem said coldly. 'I do not care which it is.'

The alien screamed again and then hurled itself at the large window at the front of the bridge. As it moved it cast off its human disguise. It had no need of a human voicebox. There was nothing to say to these petty animals. It changed back to its own form and smashed through the window, dropping lightly to the deck twenty feet below. It ran with a bizarre gait towards the front of the ship and leaped over the restraining guard rail, easily making the forty feet to its own ailing craft where it desperately scrambled inside.

Erimem paused for a moment, watching the alien vessel listing more violently and then she pushed the engines to maximum again. The Agamemnon surged forward, again driving its sharp hull into the craft, this time opening it like an egg and driving the remains beneath the surface.

'That was cold,' Ibrahim said softly. 'Their ship was probably going to sink anyway.'

'Probably was not enough,' Erimem answered. 'If there was a chance it could have sent for help from its mothership then I could not take the risk.' She sighed. 'Besides, this creature started the conflict, not us. All we could do was finish it.'

'She's right,' Helena nodded sadly. 'I wish she wasn't but she is.'

The whistle of a speaking tube interrupted the moment. Even as Andy picked it up, they could all hear shouting voices. 'Shit,' Andy muttered. 'Looks like we might be sinking.'

The *Agamemnon* did not sink. The watertight restraining doors held firm, working with the pumps to allow the stricken liner to reach port on Italy. The port's authorities were surprised to find the ship under the command of a police officer from Edinburgh. The crew were listed as having been lost or injured in the aftermath of the late night collision with an unknown vessel which had so mortally wounded the *Agamemnon*. Dr Griffiths' body had never been found, and it was assumed that the alien had thrown it overboard.

No-one would have believed the truth of what had happened and Sergeant Dorward allowed justice to take precedence over the law. Warren Anderson wrote dated cheques, forging Lord Etheridge's signature. Each cheque would allow those who had suffered under Etheridge to start again. Some of those who would thrive had done vile things, but neither Dorward nor any of Erimem's party had the appetite to act as judge and jury on individual cases – except Professor Klimt who was rightly seen as more accessory than victim. Cheques were also written to the families of the murdered crew. Despite her protests, Dorward insisted that Nadia Bakshi should also be compensated even though she was, by her own admission, quite a remarkably wealthy young woman. Helena also accepted a cheque on behalf of her party. They had followed the time traveller's first rule and opened a bank account in the past, which meant that interest and random payments had given them a healthy emergency fund. It was probably horribly immoral but none of them cared.

As the passengers from the *Agamemnon* boarded the trains which would now complete their journeys back to England, Sergeant Dorward admitted that he had broken the law and would face the consequences.

'I let Mackenzie go,' he said. 'He was a nasty piece of work but I couldn't bring myself to put him through a courts martial, because it meant that the passengers on board the ship might be called as witnesses. I put him down as being lost with the crew.' The policeman shrugged. 'His career is over, he'll have to see out his days living under an alias on the modest amount he got from Etheridge's chequebook. Arrest me if you will.'

Andy grimaced. 'Don't think I'll bother. It's been a long few days. I could do without the paperwork.'

'You have a good heart,' Erimem said. 'Make sure you harden it when you return to your work.' She glanced at Nadia. 'At least when you are on duty.'

'This sounds like you are saying goodbye,' Nadia said.

Helena nodded. 'Yeah, we have our own way home.'

'Not as romantic as a train or a boat but we do have work to get back to.'

'We will be watching the society pages, though,' Helena added. 'I'd bet you ten bob that Countess Bischkova gets her claws into Mr Hove.' The eyes of her three companions turned accusingly on her. 'Oh, all right. I remember reading, back in the day... they're do great work with refugee children in a few years after he's become Lord...' her voice tailed off sadly. 'Well, let them have a few months of happiness before that, eh?'

Dorward shook his head in confusion. 'I have no idea what you are talking about.'

'Oh, neither do I,' said Helena, forcing a smile into her voice.

'And now you must catch your train,' Erimem said. 'I wish you great success and happiness.'

'Thank you,' Nadia and Dorward said in unison. They laughed and turned away. After a few yards, she slipped her arm through his.

'Can't we take the train back as well?' Andy asked. 'I'm not in the mood for the real world yet.'

Erimem lifted her thumb and tapped the ring she wore on it. Each of them wore a similar ring, which would whisk them back through time to their home in 2019. 'Time to go home.'

EPILOGUE

Erimem met Adam Docherty on December 20th to see the *Star Wars* film, *The Rise of Skywalker*. She had seen the film twice before with Andy in trips to the future. Indeed, they had gone back to 1977 to see the original at the time of its release. Andy had worn a t-shirt with the words GREEDO SHOOTS FIRST on it.

Going to see the film with Adam was, Erimem assured everyone, not a date. He was a policeman who was assigned to deal with the university at which she, Andy and Ibrahim worked, and who had a special interest in the unusual cases surrounding the place... cases with which they were fairly inextricably linked. Adam was, she assured them, just a friend.

Nobody believed her.

'Love a bit of sci-fi,' Adam said as they settled into rather luxurious chairs at the cinema. 'My family is full of geeks.'

'You should have come with Andy,' Erimem suggested.

He smiled and she found that it was a smile she very much liked. 'I don't think I'm Andy's type,' he said meaningfully.

'Perhaps,' Erimem answered. She would go no further on her friend's sexuality. It wasn't her place to tell anyone unless Andy did so first. 'So, your father introduced you to this *Star Wars*?'

'He is totally into it,' Adam agreed, 'but it was my great grandparents who were the first big sci-fi nuts in the family. They were totally into it before it was popular.' He pulled his phone from his pocket and keyed in the security code. 'I've got a picture of them somewhere.' He handed the phone across. 'That was taken at the millennium.'

Erimem looked at the picture of an old couple, sitting together, smiling and surrounded by family. He was bald and her hair was white, contrasting with her darker skin. Through the winkles and the age she recognised the faces of Sergeant Dorward and Nadia Bakshi. In the picture, taken more than sixty years after she had last seen them, they were still holding hands.

'A mixed race couple was quite a thing back in their day,' Adam said, 'but she was royalty of some sort, grand-daughter of a Maharaja or something, and he became Detective Chief Inspector. We didn't find out they were minted until they passed away. Money wasn't a big deal for them.'

'No,' Erimem mused, 'I don't suppose it was.'

Her first thought had been one of joy that the young people she had known had lived a long and contented life together. Now, suspicions rose in her. She had no doubts that it was not a coincidence that she had helped saved the lives of Adam's great grandparents. Something had manipulated her into being there.

Was Adam involved?

Did it matter if he knew what was happening? He was involved somehow. She passed the phone back and settled into her chair, but her mind was no longer on the film. She glanced at Adam's profile, picked out by the flickering lights from the screen. Her enjoyment of the moment was gone, her trust in him unsteady.

Whatever it took, she was going to find out what was going on.

Death on the Waves

ERIMEM

A PHARAOH OF MARS

A novel by Jim Mortimore